The Underground Railroad

Books in the Choice Adventures series

The Underground Railroad

Sally Marcey

Tyndale House Publishers, Inc.
Wheaton, Illinois

Cover Illustration copyright © by Wendy Wassink Ackison
Scripture verses are taken from *The Living Bible* copyright © 1971 owned by
assignment by KNT Charitable Trust. All rights reserved.
Library of Congress Catalog Card Number 91-65080
ISBN 0-8423-5027-6
Copyright © 1991 by The Livingstone Corporation
Printed in the United States of America
98 97 96 95 94
 9   8   7   6   5

"**G**ood morning!" Willy whispered to the wooden lamb that was carved into the huge door inside old Capitol Community Church. Willy liked the way the lamb's eyes always seemed to meet his own, no matter where he stood in front of the door. He reached up and affectionately tugged the wooden lamb's ear. There was a soft click, and the hidden door in the wall swung open.

"OK, guys," he said, turning to Sam and Chris, "let's go." Willy crossed the cool stone floor of the church entry hall and stepped into the narrow stairway that could be seen behind the secret panel.

"Uh, I think we should wait for a few minutes," said Chris uncomfortably.

"For Mr. Whitehead?" asked Sam.

"No . . ." Chris hesitated.

"For Jessica," Willy said disgustedly, making a face.

"Well, it's not my fault she moved in next door, and my mother asked me to include her in our activities," said Chris defensively. "And I wasn't the one who asked her to help ring the church bell."

"No, Mr. Whitehead did," Willy grumbled. He had to admit that for the first time he was disappointed in Mr. Whitehead. Summer had been pretty exciting for Willy and the other "Ringers" ever since the Whiteheads had reopened the church at Millersburg. Days had flown by as

6

they explored the secrets of the old building and took turns making the massive bell in the tower ring. *Whoever built this old church sure knew a lot about secret passageways and hidden staircases,* Willy thought approvingly. But he wasn't so sure he liked Mr. Whitehead's inviting strangers to join the Ringers.

Actually, there was another reason Willy was acting unfriendly. This summer he had finally had some peace and quiet from the girls that always seemed to pester him at school. They tormented him with whispers and giggles that he was "so cute." His yearbook was filled with embarrassing "cute" comments. He hated that word. He wanted to be brave, daring, and maybe even do a few things this summer that were sorta scary—but definitely nothing cute! He really didn't want to hang around with girls this summer at all!

"Come on," Willy said impatiently. "We'll leave this doorway open so that Jessica can find her own way. I want to have another look around upstairs!" He disappeared up into the darkness followed by Sam.

"I don't like the idea of leaving the secret doorway open," they heard Chris call from below. "I'll wait here and bring her up."

The staircase led Willy and Sam to a long narrow room. Willy still felt the excitement of the first time he and Chris had cautiously climbed those stairs trying not to be scared. Now the room was familiar. The walls were covered with a variety of very old pictures. Some were portraits of men who must have been ministers in the old church. They were dressed in black and had long beards.

There was one picture of a young woman in a sky blue dress. When Chris had first looked at this picture, he had thought the woman looked kind of sad, as if she was watching something in the distance that she really didn't want to see.

Right next to the doorway there was a striking picture of several black men and women in gray clothing. Mr. Whitehead had told the boys that the people in the picture were Quakers. Willy always claimed that the tall black man standing in the back row looked just like his Uncle Louis.

As Willy felt along the wall of the room for the light switch Mr. Whitehead had installed, he accidentally bumped that picture and almost knocked it off the wall.

"Sorry, Uncle Louis," he said, chuckling as he tried to straighten the unsmiling group of men and women. Suddenly an old yellowed piece of paper fluttered from behind the picture.

"What's this?" said Sam as he picked it up and carefully unfolded it. They both walked to the table where Sam spread the paper out under the light. "Hey, it's a map!" he exclaimed.

"That's no map," Willy scoffed. "It's just a series of squares and squiggles."

"Squares and squiggles?" said Sam, raising his eyebrows.

"You know, like when you aren't paying attention in class so you start drawing something on a piece of paper . . ." Willy realized that Sam was much more interested in the paper than his explanation.

8

CHOICE ➡

If the boys decide that the drawing is a map, turn to page 97.

If they decide it isn't, turn to page 42.

Carefully Jessica crept away from the ladder. Where could she hide until the church service started?

"Hey, are you the new girl that moved in next door to my cousin Chris? You must be Jessica!" The voice seemed to come out of nowhere. Jessica whirled around and saw a tall girl her own age emerging from the secret staircase.

"You really scared me! Who are you?" Jessica's voice came out in a squeak.

"I'm Jill," the blond newcomer said casually. "My parents sometimes drop me off to visit Chris in the summer. You're from the city too, aren't you?"

"Yes," Jessica said hesitantly, watching the self-confident manner of the blond-haired girl before her. *I wouldn't be shy either if I looked like her,* Jessica thought.

"Aren't you going to help ring the bell?" Jill asked.

"Oh, I don't know . . ."

Jill looked at her shrewdly, "You didn't let those silly Ringers scare you away, did you?"

"Well, I . . ." Jessica couldn't meet Jill's eyes.

"Look, Jess," said Jill kindly, "I hope you don't mind being called Jess?" The other girl shook her head, and Jill went on, "I don't know what those boys did. Maybe they do act kind of weird sometimes, but they really are a lot of fun to hang around with."

"Oh, I see." Jessica tried to smile. She glanced around

the room at the pictures and the bookshelves. A hopeful thought occurred to her. "Jill, do you happen to like writing? You know, poems and stuff?"

"Not really," Jill answered. "Although I have to admit that some of the things we've found around here have been worth writing about." She stopped, then decided she might as well let this new girl know a little about herself. "My best subject in school is history, but what I really like is messing around with electricity. I've been told most girls my age find that *shocking*. I don't suppose you like wiring things and building circuits and stuff, do you?"

"No!" Jessica shuddered, not laughing at the pun.

"Oh well." Jill shrugged. "We can still be friends."

"I hope so!" Jessica said a little too fervently.

Jill gave her a curious glance. Suddenly a deep *bong, bong, bong* filled the picture room. Both girls looked up toward the attic.

"C'mon, let's take our turn ringing the bell," Jill almost shouted as she started to climb the ladder. "After all, you want to be one of the Ringers, don't you?"

Jessica smiled for real this time and followed Jill up the ladder. It wasn't much of an initiation, but she really did want to be a Ringer!

THE END

Turn to page 154.

Willy thought for a moment, then said, "Hey, we've never had decent light when we've explored before, why should we start now?"

"OK," said Sam, "but don't blame me if we don't find anything."

Because of the candle they couldn't rely on their eyesight. Instead, they slowly felt along the wall of the room with their hands. They walked along one wall, then turned a corner and felt their way along another wall, then another, and, finally, they were back again at the doorway.

"Hey," said Willy, "I guess there's no tunnel in here after all. This is just a small room, like a closet or something." He chuckled softly, then added, "See, it's all your fault, Sam!"

"Some adventure," said Sam, ignoring Willy's jab.

"Wait a minute," Chris said, "Ringers don't give up this easy. What if we read the map wrong? There are two other doors on this side of the hall—maybe the tunnel is behind one of them. Besides, we haven't really checked this room all that well."

"I guess I'm used to finding tunnels around here on the first try," admitted Willy. "But I think maybe I've spent enough time in the dark for one day. I guess we are going to need more light to find this new tunnel after all—that is if this map really is a map. Let's go to the Freeze for a treat and come back tomorrow morning."

12

But Chris really wasn't ready to give up. He could see that Sam was about ready to go too. So, he tried a last effort. "Listen, guys, let's check one more room. If that one is blank, we'll go to the Freeze."

CHOICE

If they leave, turn to page 62.

If they try Chris's suggestion first, turn to page 79.

The boys went back inside and got comfortable. Willy took care of the introductions. Great-Grandma Hattie cleared her throat and began, "You see, a long time ago our people came over to this country from Africa."

"In the slave ships," added Carla.

"Yes, in the slave ships. My granddaddy was a slave. But he didn't want to be a slave. In his heart, he wanted to be free."

"So he decided to run away," Carla interrupted.

"Let Great-Grandma tell the story, Carla," said Willy impatiently, rolling his eyes at Chris and Sam.

"That's right, child, he wanted to run away, but he was scared. You see, it was a long way to freedom, and he didn't know the way. He thought he'd be caught for sure. Slaves who were caught were punished something terrible. Sometimes, they were killed to teach other slaves a lesson!" Great-Grandma Hattie paused for a moment to catch her breath. Willy tried to imagine what it would be like to have to run away to be free. He almost laughed when he realized the only thing he could compare it to was trying to get out of the house that morning.

"Then, one night when my granddaddy was lying in his bed in the slave quarters, he heard singing. It was a woman's voice, soft and low. She was singing a song that all the slaves knew called 'Go Down Moses.'

"Well, then my granddaddy sat right up and quickly grabbed what few belongings he had and hurried to follow the singing."

"Why would he do that?" asked Chris.

"'Cause he knew what the singing meant. It meant that 'Moses' had come south again to lead some more of her people to freedom."

"Moses?" asked Sam.

"Do you remember the story of Moses in the Bible?" asked Great-Grandma Hattie. When Sam nodded, she continued, "Well there once was a woman that all the slaves called Moses. Her real name was Harriet Tubman. She walked her way to freedom in the North. But she wasn't content just to be free herself when she knew her people were in slavery. So she walked back to the South and led over three hundred slaves to freedom."

"Just like Moses led the children of Israel out of Egypt," said Sam.

"That's right, Sam," said Great-Grandma Hattie approvingly. "I can see you've been paying attention in Sunday school! So my granddaddy and the other slaves traveled with Harriet Tubman along the Underground Railroad."

"A train that traveled underground?" asked Chris.

"No, not a real railroad," Carla added importantly. "They just called it a railroad."

"The slaves often traveled at night," continued Great-Grandma, "They stayed in churches and in people's homes. They always had to be on the lookout for the slave catchers, because if the slave catchers found any runaway slaves, they would take them back to their masters and collect a big reward.

"When my granddaddy made it to freedom, he was so thankful to Moses that he named his daughter, my mama, after Moses. I was also given her name."

"Is your name Moses?" asked Sam.

Great-Grandma Hattie laughed.

"No, Sam," groaned Willy. "Great-Grandma's name is Harriet, just like Harriet Tubman's."

"Boy, that was a great story!" said Chris. "Your granddaddy must have really been brave."

"Yes, he was," said Great-Grandma. "And you boys were good listeners. Now I think maybe you're ready to have a few adventures of your own."

"Sounds good to me," said Sam, "and thanks for telling us the story!"

As the boys went out on the porch, Sam said, "Let's get to the church."

CHOICE

Turn to page 75.

"**O**K, Jess," said Chris. "Let's run up and tell Mr. Whitehead that something's in the church."

They all hurried up the basement stairs and through the sanctuary. *It's really getting dark,* Jessica thought, as she saw the fading light through the huge windows.

When they got to the door of Mr. Whitehead's study, the door was closed. They knocked and knocked, but no one answered. Cautiously, Jessica opened the door. "Mr. Whitehead?" she called. The room was empty.

"I guess he's already gone home," she said, as she turned to the boys. On their way through the sanctuary, she picked up three candles and a pack of matches that were lying on a table in the back of the church.

"Good idea," said Chris approvingly when he saw Jessica getting the candles.

"Look, this mud trail leads straight into that closet," Sam observed, pointing to a half-open doorway at the end of the hall.

"Ready, guys?" Chris asked as they took a candle. Willy lit his candle and went into the closet first. The others followed.

"There's nothing here!" said Willy disappointedly, kicking the pile of rags where the trail ended.

"Something *was* here," Sam observed, pointing to the pile of mud on the floor, "but it isn't here now. Now it looks like this mud is a two-way trail. Some kind of animal must have gotten in here."

"Now what?" Willy asked.

"It's getting late," Jessica said reluctantly. "I have to go home."

"Me too," Willy explained, "because I have to watch Carla tonight. My parents are going out. We'll have to solve this mystery some other time."

"I think we should wedge that stone doorway shut. Otherwise, we may have another mysterious visitor in the future. And let's make sure all the other doors are closed tight," said Chris, as the Ringers got ready to leave the church.

When they got outside, Jessica turned to the three boys and said shyly, "Thanks for showing me the secret slide. That was really neat!"

"Maybe tomorrow we'll get a chance to show you the room in the tunnel," Chris promised.

"That'd be great!" Jessica said happily as they all walked home together.

THE END

If you want to find out what they would have discovered if they had checked the room right away, turn to page 113.

Or, turn to page 154.

"**W**e have to talk . . . alone . . . for a minute, Jess," said Chris as he pulled Willy a little way off from the girl.

"What's there to talk about?" grumbled Willy.

"Hey, c'mon, Willy," Chris nudged his friend. "She showed us the diary, didn't she?"

"You know how I feel about girls," Willy muttered. "But you're right. She did show us the diary. OK, we'll show her the slide in the attic, but that's all for now."

"Alright," Chris agreed.

They turned toward the girl who looked like she had been left on a deserted island. "Let's go," said Chris, gesturing and smiling at Jessica as they walked toward the old church. "We'll show you one of our favorite secret passageways." She followed them, shaking her head in wonder.

Once they had decided to show her the tunnel, they found it was exciting to let someone experience it for the first time. Both Chris and Willy still remembered vividly their discovery of that dark and surprising place.

"The place to start is in the attic," announced Willy as they approached the front door of the church. "We found a secret tunnel that leads straight down to the basement."

"Maybe," said Chris as he thought about the diary, "that slide is more than just a neat way to slide down through the building. Maybe slaves used that passageway to escape when the church was being searched."

"Oh, I can't wait!" giggled Jessica enthusiastically.

Willy gave Chris a this-was-your-idea look and pulled the lamb's ear. They climbed the secret staircase, then scrambled up the ladder into the attic. Jessica was enjoying herself. She still couldn't believe Chris and Willy were actually letting her in on one of their secrets. Maybe they would let her be a Ringer after all!

But a few moments later, she definitely had some second thoughts when she peered down the dark, narrow hole that Willy pointed out next to the chimney in the attic floor.

"What's down there?" she asked, trying not to sound afraid.

"Oh, there's your usual assortment of spiders and crawly things," Willy mentioned calmly. Her shudder gave him the expected response.

"Willy's just kidding," said Chris. "He hates spiders as much as anybody. Now, in this top part of the tunnel, there are steps built into the wall, Jess," Chris explained reassuringly. "All you have to do is climb down. When the steps end, there's kind of a slide that goes into the basement."

"But if you think it's too scary," Willy added, "just go back down the stairs to the church basement, and we'll meet you there."

Obviously, Jessica was not going to admit she was scared, even though she was terrified. She hated the dark. She even kept a small light on in her room at night. But she

20

realized that she had to prove herself to the boys if she had any hope of hanging out with them. So she gritted her teeth and followed Chris down into the darkness.

No sooner had she gotten down in the tunnel, she heard Chris say from below, "There's a short drop between the bottom of the steps and the slide, Jess. You have to hang by your hands, then let go. The slide will do the rest." Then his voice rapidly faded as he yelled, "See you in a little bit . . ."

Jess counted the rungs in the wall, carefully reaching for each one with her foot. *Sixteen, seventeen, eighteen* . . . Then there was nothing but air. She realized she had come to the end of the ladder and the moment of truth. Moments later she was hanging from her hands with her toes barely touching the slide. Her hands didn't seem to want to obey her. She made a little whimper of frustration.

"Oh, c'mon," said Willy impatiently from above. "If you're too scared, why don't you climb back up?"

That did it. Jessica let go. As soon as her feet settled on the slide, the slippery, steeply slanted surface took control. She screamed as she picked up speed, then tumbled out onto the basement floor. Chris was laughing. She sat up with her hair in her eyes. For a split second, she thought he was laughing at her, but then she realized he was enjoying the fun she had just had. She began chuckling too.

Chris calmly said, "Move over and watch this!"

His timing was perfect. No sooner had Jess moved than a sound like a locomotive whistle filled the hallway. The wall panel opened, and Willy flew from the chute. He rolled head over heels across the floor, laughing all the way.

"That gets better every time!" he whooped.

In no time at all they were back in the attic for another trip. As they laughed together, the boys seemed to forget who Jessica was. She felt included.

After a couple of slides, the boys told her about their first time down. They talked about finding Miss Whitehead's room with things she had written on the blackboard before she died. They all talked about ways the tunnel might have been used to help slaves.

The morning went as fast as it usually does when you're having a good time. Willy glanced at his watch as he was dusting himself off and said, "I'd better get home. It's almost lunchtime."

"Wanna do something this afternoon?" Chris asked his friend.

"Can't," Willy explained. "I have to mow the lawn and do some yard work for my dad."

As they made their way to the door, Jess said quietly, "Thanks for showing me the secret tunnel."

"That's OK," mumbled Willy. He wasn't about to admit that having a girl along all morning hadn't been that bad. Outside, they went their separate ways.

For Jessica, the morning had been wonderful. She hadn't gotten so dirty in a long time. She hadn't gotten in *their* way, either. Things they had said let her know there were a lot more secrets to learn about in the church. Maybe she could help. She might even become a Ringer!

22

THE END

Turn to page 154.

I wish I'd found a secret room, Jessica thought despondently as she walked home. When she got there, she fixed herself some lunch, then took the diary to her room to read. But lunch and a late night the previous evening caught up with her, and she fell asleep.

She dreamed that she was running back and forth in the basement of the church, checking rooms over and over. She woke up when her dad got home from work.

"I wasn't sure you'd be home yet, Jess. Did you have a good time?"

"It was OK, I guess," Jessica mumbled. And then without warning, she burst into tears.

As her dad's arms closed around her, Jess sobbed, "I really didn't want to move here, Dad. None of the other kids like me. I didn't really have a friend to visit, I just told you I had one so I could go exploring without you worrying about me . . ."

Jessica's dad waited until she finished crying and then said, "I know it's been tough for you to have to move, Sweetheart. Tell you what, I don't have to work tomorrow, so maybe we can take some time and check out this little town together."

"Thanks, Dad. That'd be great," Jessica sighed.

"And Mrs. Martin from next door tells me that her niece, Jill, is coming to visit for the rest of the summer. Finally you'll have a girl to hang around with instead of those awful boys!" Jessica's dad made a face as he said the word *boys,* and Jessica laughed through her tears.

"Oh, Daddy. Don't make me laugh. Besides, they're not *that* bad. It's just that I feel like I get in their way," she said.

Jessica wasn't sure if she would be friends with Chris's cousin, Jill, but the promise of spending a day with her dad certainly cheered her up. Later that night, as she climbed into bed, she pulled out a small blank book from beneath the mattress and began to write:

> *July 3, Millersburg*
> *So far I haven't found a friend, but I did find a neat diary written around 1851. I discovered that the church here was once a station for the Underground Railroad. I checked the basement of the church today for any secret rooms, but didn't find any. They may have been destroyed, or maybe I just wasn't looking in the right places. Wonder how much the Ringers know . . . Sure is scary doing this alone. Tomorrow I am going to spend a day with my dad, and we'll probably go to a park and then maybe eat out for lunch . . .*

In spite of her nap, she was very tired. She put her diary away and snuggled down in the covers. As she drifted off to sleep she wondered if anyone would ever find her diary exciting to read.

THE END

Turn to page 154.

Willy wrote a note in big letters to Carla. The note read:

> *Dear Carla,*
>
> > *Grandmother's not coming today. I went to meet Sam and Chris. I'll be home by 9:30. Stay inside until I come home.*
>
> > *Willy*

Then Willy took a box of Carla's favorite cereal out of the cabinet and propped the note against the cereal box on the kitchen counter. He placed a bowl and spoon beside the box. He found an emergency candle and a box of matches in the miscellaneous drawer. Quietly he opened the door and made sure to lock it again with his key before he ran as quickly as he could to the old church.

When he got to the church, no one was around. Willy tried to open the secret door on the side of the church, but at first it wouldn't budge. He really pushed hard on the stones, and finally the door gave way. He almost fell down the stairs like his friend Pete had done the first time they discovered this hidden entrance to the church. A section of foundation stones had actually been made into a door that opened onto a flight of stairs leading down. They had found it completely by accident . . . but that's another story.

He sat on the top stone step and prepared to light his candle. The matches he had brought turned out to be one match left in the box. He had been in such a hurry that he hadn't even shaken the box to check. Willy mumbled something to himself about this not being his day and lit the candle.

In the light of his candle Willy noticed several things right away. The door at the bottom of the steps that led into the church basement was closed tightly. To its right, he could see that the other door at the bottom of the stairs that led to the secret tunnel was ajar.

"Hey, Sam . . . Chris . . . are you guys down there?" Willy called softly.

No one answered. Willy slid down the stairs, sitting on each step. He tugged on the basement door and found that it wouldn't open. It usually slid up easily like a garage door. He swallowed hard. Gently, he pushed open the other door. It was really dark in the stairwell.

"Hey, Sam, Chris, it's Willy," he called a little louder.

Still there was no answer except the echo of his voice. Willy carefully went down a few steps. He was listening hard. He thought he heard some faint scuffling noises down in the tunnel. *The gang must be exploring after all,* he thought. *They're making enough noise that they can't hear me.* He tried to stand up. That was another mistake. He brushed the same stone Sam moved during their first trip in the tunnel, and the door behind him swung shut.

Willy looked down just in time to see the flame on his candle point toward the moving door, then go out. Darkness swallowed everything.

Willy's first thought was to scream at the top of his lungs. How many things could go wrong in one morning?

His next breath was a lungful of candle smoke. He coughed out his friends' names again, this time louder. No one answered. At the sound of his voice, though, the faint noises he had been hearing stopped.

Willy was beginning to feel more than a little worried. Sam and Chris would have answered him by this time. He thought about leaving Carla all alone at home when his mother had told him to watch her. Suddenly, this was the last place he wanted to be.

Why hadn't he had Sam show him exactly how to open the door? Now he was trapped. The only way out was through the tunnel. As he stopped to catch his breath, the scuffling sounds he had heard in the tunnel suddenly started again. He didn't know what to do. He realized he could go down the stairs and see who was in the tunnel. Or, he could stay as quiet as possible right where he was and wait for help to come. Surely either Chris or Sam would figure out sooner or later where he was!

CHOICE ⟹

If Willy investigates the noises, turn to page 107.

If Willy waits at the top of the stairs, turn to page 146.

Sam opened the envelope and pulled out a torn piece of paper. It looked like a note. He read the hand-printed words several times, but the words just didn't make sense.

"Hey, guys," he said, "I found something, but I'm not sure what it is."

"Is it another map?" asked Willy hopefully, forgetting that Jessica might hear. But she was too absorbed in her own discovery to pay any attention to what he was saying.

"No," Sam said, "it's a letter or something."

"What's it say?" asked Chris.

Sam began to read:

> *John,*
>
> > *Deliver all pieces of baggage to the livery stable one hour after sunset. Leonard Grimes is leaving tonight on the Railroad for Philadelphia. Room for six passengers. Keep thee safe.*

"Weird!" exclaimed Chris. "I can't figure it out."

CHOICE ⇶

Can you figure out what the letter means? Turn to page 53 for some more clues.

"**W**hat's that?" asked Willy.

"To begin with," said Mrs. Turner, "all of this is part of the history of our nation. But even more important for us is seeing how Christians have made a difference in our country by helping others. I'm pretty sure that you haven't heard much in school about the way the Christian faith has shaped our nation all along the way, but kids your age need a chance to learn that. People who followed Jesus Christ made some real sacrifices for others because they felt that's what Jesus would want them to do. People in Willy's family and my family gained their freedom that way. One of the reasons I became a Christian myself is because I began to discover from history how much I owed to Christians in the past. That led me to find out how much I owed to Christ. In a sense, I've discovered that Christians helped my family gain social freedom, and Jesus Christ set me completely free."

For the next several hours, the Ringers told Mrs. Turner about their adventures in the church and the discoveries they had made. They even mentioned the map they'd found. Mrs. Turner was doubtful that people would have gone to the trouble of digging two tunnels when so much had gone into the one they had found.

Chris pulled out the map and showed it to her. "Well," said Mrs. Turner, "it looks old enough, but it may have been two choices for the original tunnel. Let me know if you find anything."

Chris was relieved she hadn't wanted to look for the tunnel with them. He liked the idea of the Ringers being in charge of making new discoveries around the church.

Mrs. Turner interrupted his thinking with a question for all of them. "Have you figured out how to get the other door in this room open? It must lead to a way out."

The kids had tried several times. But the door was very thick and well built. The massive lock had done its work so far.

That lock reminds me of something, thought Willy. Maybe it was because they had just been telling someone all their other discoveries around the old church that a piece of the puzzle fell in place for him. He shouted suddenly, "I got it!" and ran out of the room. The others sat there stunned.

Willy was back moments later with a big smile on his face. "Remember, Chris and Jill, when we tried to open that locked door upstairs when we first started exploring? On the molding above the door we found a big, old key that wouldn't fit the door? Well, I put it back up there later, and I just went to get it. I think it might just fit this lock." He had been moving across the room as he explained, so that he finished talking just as he pushed the key into the slot in the lock. It fit. He turned the key and felt the lock give a rusty squeak as it slid open.

They all gathered around in anticipation as Willy twisted the door handle. He didn't have to pull the door open. As soon as the handle moved far enough the door

32

swung hard in Willy's direction like there was someone leaning against it. They all jumped back in shock as dirt poured through the opening into the room.

"Cave in!" shouted Sam and turned toward the way out.

But the excitement was over as suddenly as it began. The pyramid of dirt in the doorway was the end of the cave in. Mr. Whitehead looked around and noticed again how massive the beams were that held the roof of the room and the tunnel. He shook his head and said, "I guess we won't find out how they got out this way now that the tunnel has caved in. I'm just glad something like that didn't happen while we were exploring."

Though there seemed to be no immediate danger, it suddenly seemed like a good idea to go somewhere else. Mrs. Turner had a suggestion. "Since you've been such a big help with my research, can I offer you something at that ice cream place I noticed across the park?" She laughed at the five vigorously nodding heads gathered around her.

THE END

Turn to page 154.

The next morning, Willy lost no time in getting out of bed and getting dressed. He closed his bedroom door softly and tiptoed past his sister's room. Through the open doorway, he could see his six-year-old sister Carla sound asleep, hugging Moses, her big stuffed bear, next to her cheek.

Willy smiled. He really liked Carla. Even though she was a girl, she was a good sport. She was really good at keeping secrets and, most important, she didn't try to get him into trouble with Mom or Dad when he teased her. But today, he didn't want Carla to wake up and try to tag along with him when he was going to explore the secret passageways of the old church.

I hope Chris remembers to bring the map, he thought as he snuck down the stairs. He tried to walk like an Indian, stepping so quietly that he wouldn't make a sound. He had just started to unlock the front door when he heard his mother's voice from the kitchen.

"Good morning, Son. You're up early this morning." Willy's mom stepped into the hall. Willy saw that she was all dressed for work.

"Morning, Mom," Willy called cheerfully as he turned to go out the door. "Have a good day at work. Could you tell Grandmother I'll be home by lunchtime?"

"Wait a minute, Willy," said his mother. "Where are you going at this hour of the morning?"

"I, ah, I'm just going out to meet the guys."

"At 6:30 A.M.? That's a little early, don't you think?" his mom asked. "And Willy, your grandmother isn't coming here today. She's gone to visit Great-Grandma Hattie. You'll have to take care of Carla for me until this afternoon."

"But Mom, not today! I've already made plans with Sam and Chris." Willy looked pleadingly at his mom.

"Sorry, Willy," his mother said firmly, "but today I need you to help me out while I'm at work."

"Aw, Mom," Willy tried again, "couldn't Carla play at one of her friend's houses today? I really have to meet the guys this morning. They're probably waiting for me already!"

"No, Willy. I'm sorry you have to change your plans, but today you'll have to take care of Carla. I think your friends will understand."

"OK, Mom," Willy mumbled and climbed the stairs back to his room. He sat on the edge of his bed and thought about all the fun that the others were going to have exploring the old church. He thought back to the beginning of the summer when he and Chris had first heard that bell in the old church ring and had decided to investigate. What neat adventures they had had! And now, even though he had been the one to find the map, he was stuck at home watching his sister.

Willy heard his mother's car pull out of the garage. He got up and peeked into Carla's room. She was still asleep. She looked really tired.

"I bet I can go to the church and meet the guys, then come back before Carla even wakes up," he said to himself. "Mom did tell me to take care of Carla, and if she finds out that I didn't stay home, I'll really be in trouble. But I'll come right back and play games with Carla for the rest of the day! After all, I did give Sam and Chris my word that I'd meet them at the church."

CHOICE

If Willy leaves Carla a note and meets his friends at the church, turn to page 26.

If Willy stays home with his sister and misses exploring the secret tunnel, turn to page 71.

"**Y**ou're right," she whispered to the lamb. "I'll return the diary." She started to reach for the lamb's ear when something crashed loudly in the room above her. It sounded as if something was falling through the ceiling!

Someone else was in the church! Jessica froze in panic for a moment. She couldn't hear anything else except the pounding of her heart in her ears.

"I've got to get out of here!" she murmured, as she spun and stepped toward the outside door. "On the way home, I'll tell Mr. Whitehead that someone is in the church. They might be trying to steal something."

Just as she was pushing on the door, she heard a faint noise through the ceiling above her. The noise sounded like someone saying, "Help me . . ."

Did someone call for help, or was I just imagining it? she asked herself as she ran down the church steps. As much as she wanted to believe she had imagined the cry for help, she knew it was real. Someone needed help. *What should I do?* she asked herself.

CHOICE ⟹

If Jessica goes to Mr. Whitehead's house for help, turn to page 87.

If she goes up the staircase to see who's there, turn to page 49.

Chris climbed down the fire escape and snuck around behind Jill so that she couldn't see him. Then he moved quietly right behind her and said in a low, deep voice, "Hello, Jill."

Jill shrieked and whirled around. "Oh Chris, you creep, you really scared me!" she said catching her breath.

"What're you doing here?"

"I've been trying to find you guys," Jill exclaimed breathlessly. "I went to the Freeze after my parents dropped me off at your house, and Betty told me you were on some wild chase after some man and boy who were acting strange. She thought you had gone down Oak Street. I just guessed you would have ended up down at this end of town."

Chris had to admit it was a pretty good guess. He told her about their suspicions and the milk carton picture.

"Wow, maybe the boy was kidnapped!" Jill exclaimed. "Is this really him?" Out of her back pocket she pulled a folded panel from a milk carton. "Betty thought this might come in handy if you guys saw the kid again. There's a number to call, too. Do you think we ought to tell the police?"

"Right now Sam and Willy are hiding in the old furniture factory." Chris pointed to the old building across the street. "Let's go over and get them. Then we can decide what to do."

"I really think we should talk to the police," Jill said, as she and Chris climbed the fire escape to the furniture factory. Jill was glad that she had found her cousin. He always seemed to know what to do, especially if there was trouble.

Chris, Jill, Willy, and Sam talked over their options. They all agreed that things definitely looked serious and that a rescue attempt had to be planned.

"But first, I'm sure we should go to the police!" Jill insisted.

"But we can do other things, too," Willy argued. "Somebody's gotta stay here and watch. That way we'll know if anybody goes in or out of that apartment. If the man leaves, we might even have a chance to rescue the boy."

"OK," Chris decided. "Willy, you and Sam stay here while Jill and I go to the police station. We'll come back as soon as we can."

CHOICE ⇒

If you want to go to the police station with Jill and Chris, turn to page 101.

If you want to stay with Willy and Sam, turn to page 150.

The boys stayed back from the window in the factory and waited several minutes. When they finally looked out the window again, Jill was gone.

"I wonder why she was here?" asked Chris.

"Maybe we should have talked to her to find out," said Sam.

The boys stayed a while longer in the factory, but they didn't see anything at all unusual or strange going on in the apartment building across the street.

"OK, guys, I've had about enough. How about you?" Willy said about an hour later. This was definitely not his idea of how to spend an exciting afternoon.

"Me, too," said Sam. "I'm just not sure anymore that the kid we saw was the same one on the milk carton. Let's go back to the Freeze and get those milk shakes we left behind."

"I guess that's all right with me, too," said Chris, turning to leave.

Seconds after the boys left the factory, a frightened white face peered out of the second-story apartment window across the street. Suddenly the face vanished, as if its owner had been yanked roughly back into the room.

The three boys bounded down the fire escape stairs, raced down Pine Street and cut through the empty field and past the old church to the Freeze. When they burst through the door, Betty pulled the milk shakes she had begun for them out of the cooler. "I had a feeling you boys would be back sooner or later for these," she chuckled. They never realized how close they came to being heroes that day.

THE END

If you think the boys made a mistake giving up so easily, turn to page 38.

If you want to join them on a different adventure, turn to page 104 or page 63.

42

As soon as the words came out of Willy's mouth, he realized, *Of course it was a map! Who would hide a page of doodles under an old picture?* He got excited and hoped they really had found a map.

CHOICE

Turn to page 97.

It didn't take Willy and Chris long to resume their places in the furniture factory. The hours dragged by.

"This is starting to feel like home," Willy joked as he pulled an old box up next to the window. "Today I remembered to bring some cards."

Chris and Willy played three games of War and one of Crazy Eights when all of a sudden, the door to the apartment building opened.

As Chris and Willy watched, the strange man left the apartment building. He was holding tightly onto the boy beside him. Chris and Willy couldn't see the boy's face.

"Let's find out what's going on!" Chris cried, jumping up and running toward the fire escape.

"Now's our chance!" yelled Willy as he and Chris scrambled down the fire escape stairs and raced to the front of the building. The man saw them coming across the street, and he looked at them with an angry expression on his face. At that moment, Willy noticed Jill and Sam coming toward them from the opposite direction. He also saw a police car come around the corner beyond them.

Chris yelled, "Hey, Mister. We want to ask you something!"

The roof lights on the squad car began to flash.

44

CHOICE ⟹

If you haven't read Jill and Sam's experience, turn to page 57.

If you already have, turn to page 128.

"**I** don't care what they think about me," Jessica said to herself. But deep down inside, she really did care, very much. Before she lost her courage, she quickly climbed the ladder to the attic.

When she got to the top of the ladder, she ignored the three boys standing there and instead concentrated on Mr. Whitehead's smile. He, at least, seemed glad to see her.

"Good morning, Jess. Why don't you take the first turn ringing the bell? Ladies first, you know!" said Mr. Whitehead, winking at Willy who smothered a groan.

Jessica reached out for the rope and grabbed it firmly with both hands. She began to count silently and then pulled the rope hard—one-rest, two-rest, three-rest . . .

Jessica forgot that the boys were there. She even forgot that she was too tall and that she hadn't wanted to move to Millersburg or even that she was up early on Sunday to go to church. All she thought about was reaching up and pulling the heavy rope again, and again, and again, as the wonderful *bong, bong, bong* vibrated through the bell tower and all around the attic.

Reluctantly, Jessica passed the rope to Willy, who took his turn. Then Sam and finally Chris took a turn. At last, as the five of them left the attic to go to the sanctuary, the bell was silent.

Downstairs, the church was quiet too, with just a few

families seated for morning worship. Jessica stole a glance at Mr. Whitehead, now seated at the front of the church. He didn't seem disappointed, or at least he didn't show it. He met her eyes and smiled warmly. Jessica ducked her head and stared at the floor.

She wondered why the man leading the service asked everyone to call him Mr. Whitehead, and not Pastor Whitehead. It seemed strange. She would have to ask him sometime. When the Scripture reading was announced, Jess lifted a Bible from the pew rack in front of her and opened to Hebrews 12:1-2. She followed as the verses were read by Willy's dad, who was helping Mr. Whitehead with the service that day. Mr. Washington read in his booming voice:

"Since we have such a huge crowd of men of faith watching us from the grandstands, let us strip off anything that slows us down or holds us back, and especially those sins that wrap themselves so tightly around our feet and trip us up; and let us run with patience the particular race that God has set before us. Keep your eyes on Jesus, our leader and instructor."

Next, Mr. Whitehead got up and began to explain what the verses meant. He talked about Christians who have already died watching us from heaven and cheering for us. He even mentioned his sister, whom Jess had already heard Chris and Willy mention several times. She had been their Sunday school teacher until she had died a couple of years before. As Mr. Whitehead ended his talk, he said, "I'm sure my sister is standing in heaven just as close as she can to Jesus, and they're all watching us this morning, hoping we'll do our very best to live for Christ!"

Jess wasn't sure she understood it all, but it was interesting. The Whiteheads were really caring people. During the service, Jessica couldn't help looking around at the old church and dreaming about all the different kinds of people that might have come here in the past. She made up some stories in her mind about the people she had seen on the walls of the picture room. The bell's ringing kept echoing in her mind.

At one point in the sermon, Jessica noticed that her dad was listening closely to what Mr. Whitehead was saying. Jessica wondered when she saw the sad expression on his face. *He's probably missing Mom again,* she thought.

Soon it was time for Sunday school. Jessica was the only girl. She moved her chair a little bit away from the boys because she didn't think they would want to sit beside her. Chris turned to her and said, almost kindly, "I think my cousin Jill will be around by next Sunday." Then he ran out of things to say.

During the lesson, Mrs. Whitehead talked about Jesus being the Good Shepherd and that we are God's sheep. Jessica was daydreaming and didn't really listen.

Later, when Jessica had to say her memory verse for Mrs. Whitehead, she imagined that the bell was still ringing, and she said her verse in time to the bell's rhythm.

"Whew, I'm glad that's over with!" said Willy after he finished his verse.

"You all did very well!" said Mrs. Whitehead. "I'll see you next week."

"Let's go," Willy said to Sam. "Are you coming, Chris?"

"In a minute," said Chris. "You guys go on ahead."

Chris waited until Willy and Sam were gone, and then he turned to Jessica. "Do you want to walk home with us?" he asked hesitantly.

Jessica glanced at Chris quickly and then looked down again. He really looked uncomfortable. She knew he didn't really want her to hang around with him, but it would be kind of nice for a change not to be by herself.

CHOICE ⟹

If Jessica walks home with Chris and the other guys, turn to page 131.

If Jessica walks home by herself, turn to page 90.

Reluctantly Jessica turned around, entered the church, and tugged the lamb's ear. When the secret door swung open, she took a deep breath and called up the stairs. Her voice wasn't very steady.

"Hello, is anybody up there?"

There was no answer.

Now what? she wondered as she inched up the stairs. Her knees felt as if they would collapse at any moment. Her heart was pounding as she reached the last curve in the staircase.

I wish I knew how to pray! she thought, as she peeked around the door to the picture room. She gasped! Willy was sprawled out on the floor under a very large box. He was trying feebly to push it off himself.

"Willy, are you OK?" she cried as she struggled to pull the box off him.

"I guess so," Willy said, looking kind of dazed as he tried to sit up. "I was trying to climb down from the attic with this box when my foot slipped and I, oh, *ow!*" Willy moaned as he tried to move his leg.

Jessica watched Willy grimace in pain, and her heart sank. *He probably broke his leg when he fell,* she thought.

"Where's the phone?" she asked. "I'll call for help."

"There isn't any," Willy groaned, lying back down. His leg was hurting so badly that he didn't really want to talk.

I'll have to run and get help, Jessica thought as she looked helplessly at Willy and saw that he was brushing away tears.

Suddenly she had an idea. The bell! Quickly she climbed up the ladder to the attic and rang the bell. She gave three short pulls, stopped, then three more short pulls. Somewhere she had read that three of anything is a help code.

Then she climbed back down the ladder and leaned over to squeeze Willy's shoulder, "Hang on, Willy, I'll be back as soon as I can," she said and hurried down the stairs.

Jessica raced out of the church, and, amazingly, she saw Chris and Sam already running toward her across the Common! She met them across the street.

"We were going into the Freeze, when we heard the bell . . ." Chris called out.

"I'm glad you heard and understood! Willy fell from the attic ladder and got hurt," Jessica panted.

"Let's go," Sam blurted out, as he sprinted toward the church. Chris was right on his heels.

Just then Mr. Whitehead's car pulled up to the curb.

"Is there trouble?" he asked. "I heard the bell when I was going to the post office, and I thought—"

"Willy fell upstairs," Jessica said urgently. "I think his leg's hurt."

The four of them rushed up the narrow stairs to find that Willy had propped himself up against the wall. He was sitting there with a weak grin on his face. "Sorry about all this," was all he could think of to say.

Mr. Whitehead was anxious to know what had happened and how badly Willy was hurt.

"Would you believe I was attacked from behind by that guard-box?" Willy said, pointing to the box Jessica had helped lift off him. The others smiled their relief to hear that their friend's sense of humor hadn't been damaged in the fall. "It wasn't the fall that hurt the most," explained Willy. "It was the ankle twist just before the fall that still doesn't feel great at all!"

After a while, Willy thought he could probably get downstairs with a little help. He had insisted they shouldn't call anyone else. "If any more people know about this secret stairway, we're gonna have to put a sign downstairs that says Open to the Public!" Willy pointed out. With some grunts, groans, and giggling, they got him standing. He put his arm around Chris's shoulder for support. The others went down the stairs in front of them, trying to help. In spite of Willy's pain, they were in light spirits.

Halfway down the stairs, Sam said, "Maybe we should all fall down. That way we can get a group discount at the hospital!"

It turned out Willy had sprained his ankle badly and had to be on crutches for almost a month. Eventually, he learned to do several tricks with his crutches, and they didn't slow him up much either. But he did have to sit for a while each day, and he actually spent time reading, even books about history. And amazingly enough, the person who cheered him up the most was Jessica!

52

THE END

Turn to page 154.

"What is it, Jessica?" asked Willy.

"It's an old diary," Jessica exclaimed, skipping
through some of the pages at the beginning of the book.
"I can't read all of the handwriting, but listen to this!"

> *October 8, 1851*
> *Picked up three large packages and two
> small ones. All were very cold. Used up
> all the old clothing. Have to ask ladies in
> sewing group for some more, especially warm
> coats.*
>
> *October 22, 1851*
> *John got back today very late from the next
> station. Fortunately we have heard that Ezra
> and Joshua were delivered safely to freedom!
> Praise be to God and to our brother Thomas
> Garrett!*
>
> *October 25, 1851*
> *Sunday services. How sad to not be able to
> worship together. We are all his people, the
> sheep of his pasture.*

"That was part of our Bible verse," Willy pointed out.

"Don't you get it?" cried Jessica.

"Get what?" asked Sam.

"Don't you guys know anything about history?"
Jessica muttered. She read the next entry.

October 31, 1851
Schooled our eleven packages today.
Another close call! Slave catchers searched the
church and found nothing. Almost caught
everyone upstairs, though. Jim's chute worked
perfectly. They searched from bottom to top.
Meanwhile, the packages went the other way.
This new law has made criminals of us all!

"Slave catchers?" exclaimed Willy.

"Yes!" said Jessica excitedly, "Whoever wrote this diary was helping slaves escape! This diary is all about the Underground Railroad."

"My Great-Grandma Hattie talks about the Underground Railroad!" said Willy importantly. "Grandma Hattie's grandfather was a slave and he escaped on the Railroad. Let me see that book!"

Jessica handed the book to Willy, who began to leaf through it.

"I wonder," Chris said thoughtfully, "if this church was a station on the Railroad?"

"Maybe that's why a secret stairway leads to the 'picture room,'" said Sam, "because the slaves were hiding here."

"Maybe." Chris continued, "I wonder if the slaves were hidden in that earth room that we found in the tunnel."

"What room in the tunnel?" Jessica asked with interest. The tunnel under the church had been discovered by the Ringers in an earlier adventure. They all realized they now had a very curious girl on their hands.

At that moment, the Ringers heard a familiar voice call from the foot of the staircase. "Jessica, are you up there?"

"It's Mr. Whitehead," Sam whispered.

Jessica raised her voice, "Yes, I'm up here with Willy, Sam, and Chris." She stood up and walked over to the top of the stairs. "We're exploring the picture room."

"That's fine." Mr. Whitehead's voice floated up the stairs. "I'll be in my study doing a little reading." They heard his muffled footsteps retreating through the church sanctuary toward his study.

"Let's show this book to Mr. Whitehead," Willy suggested, waving the diary. "He might be able to tell us something more about this church being a station for the Railroad."

"Let's explore on our own a little first," said Sam. "We can show Jessica the room in the tunnel we found."

CHOICE ⇒

If they go to the room in the tunnel, turn to page 68.

If they go talk to Mr. Whitehead, turn to page 83.

56

Willy said, "I guess we could use a flashlight, but I think all three of us should go get it."

That seemed fair enough to Chris and Sam, so they left the church the way they had entered. As they were closing the stone door, Chris's cousin Jill showed up. She came to town each summer to spend time at Chris's house and get away from the city. But she was several days early.

"I came early because my parents said I could have my birthday here and invite all of you out for pizza!" she announced.

Suddenly, the urgency to look for the new tunnel didn't seem like such a big deal. But an offer of free all-you-can-eat pizza doesn't come along every day. The boys briefly told Jill what they had been doing, but they decided that the party would be the priority this day, and the map would wait for tomorrow.

Willy chuckled and said, "Whether it's a map or squiggles, it won't hurt to wait another day."

THE END

Turn to page 154.

Jill caught up with Sam, and they walked around Millersburg. Sam thought the whole idea was pretty stupid, but Jill was quite serious about "detective work" as she called it. Actually, they spent most of their time in the Freeze.

"It's been three hours," Sam said finally, "and we haven't seen anything very strange. Let's go back to the factory and talk to Willy and Chris."

Jill had to agree. The morning had been a real disappointment. They were about to leave the ice cream shop when Officer Gary drove up in his squad car. He was in a hurry.

"Hi, Jill. Hi, Sam. I've been looking for you kids. Should have known to look here first," he said. "Where are Willy and Chris?"

After a brief hesitation, Sam blurted out, "They're down at the factory still watching the place where the man took the kid. Chris wouldn't give up saying something was wrong."

"Well, for once I'm glad Chris is stubborn," said Officer Gary. "Come on. I may need you as witnesses. I'll explain in the car." The policeman told them quickly that there had been a terrible mistake about the names and pictures on the milk cartons. The boy named Trent Gallagher had been found, but it wasn't his picture on the milk carton. That picture was of Mike Trent. The names and pictures had gotten mixed up. "So, you guys may have spotted a missing child after all," he said as they pulled up near the corner of Oak Street and Pine.

"I may have to chase this guy," said the officer, "so I can't have you in the squad car. You'll have to walk from here."

Sam and Jill got out and began to walk toward the factory. Officer Gary paused a moment to radio his location to the station. Imagine the kids' surprise when they turned the corner to discover the strange man just up the street coming their way! He had the little boy by the arm and was looking over his shoulder at Chris and Willy who were just crossing the street on the run.

They heard Chris yell, "Hey, Mister! We want to ask you something!"

CHOICE ⇒

If you haven't read about Chris and Willy's experience, turn to page 43.

If you have, turn to page 128.

The next morning, Jessica wasn't exactly sure if she was going to show the diary to the boys or not, but she decided that she would "if the opportunity presented itself." Her grandfather had always said those words, and Jessica liked how they sounded.

She really missed her grandfather. It had been two years since he had died. Sometimes, Mr. Whitehead reminded Jessica of her grandfather. She supposed it was because he was also kind.

So Jessica put the diary into her purse and went outside. She checked Chris's apartment, but he wasn't around. Jessica had no exact direction in mind; she ended up wandering toward the old church. She was almost there when she saw Willy and Chris coming toward her.

"Hi, Jessica," Chris mumbled. Willy didn't say anything.

"Hi, guys," she said as she kept on going.

"Where do you think she's headed?" Willy asked as he watched Jessica walk away from them.

"Looks like she's going to the church."

"Hey, Jessica, wait up," Chris called as he hurried to catch up with Jessica.

Jessica stopped for a moment and let Chris catch up.

"What's up?" Chris asked casually. Jessica couldn't help but notice how cute he looked with his blond hair falling over his forehead. *His eyes are really blue!* she thought.

Suddenly Jessica didn't want to keep the secret of the diary any longer.

"I found an old book yesterday afternoon in the picture room. It's a diary, written around 1851. There's some stuff in it about the Underground Railroad," she said, pulling the diary out of her purse.

"What's the Underground Railroad?" asked Chris.

"I know," said Willy, who had been holding back. His curiosity got the best of him. "The Underground Railroad wasn't a real railroad. That was just what people called the route that the slaves took to freedom. Thousands of slaves escaped from the South to the North back then. The houses where the slaves hid were called 'stations,' and the people who helped the slaves were called 'conductors.'"

"When did you start to like history?" Chris asked him, raising an eyebrow. "That was some lecture, Professor!"

Willy ignored his teasing. "My great-great-great-grandfather was a passenger!" he said proudly.

"Wow!" Jessica exclaimed. "That's really neat!"

She handed the diary to the boys. Willy and Chris glanced through the book together.

"Jess, I'd like to show this book to my Great-Grandma Hattie! She knows a lot about the railroad," said Willy.

"I think the church was used as a station," Jessica declared.

"That would explain the secret staircase and the passageways," Chris said thoughtfully.

"Secret passageways?" asked Jessica, beginning to feel excited.

"We found a few of them when we were first exploring the church," Chris admitted despite the look Willy was giving him.

"Oh, could you show me some?" Jessica asked eagerly.

CHOICE ⇒

If the boys show Jessica the secret passageways and tunnels that they have already discovered, turn to page 18.

If they don't tell her their secrets, turn to page 137.

"**C**ome on, guys," Sam said, "let's go get some ice cream. We can save this room for another time." Sam and Willy turned to go.

"But—," Chris began, then let out a frustrated sigh. Sam and Willy weren't negotiating. He followed them out of the tunnels and over to the Freeze, where Chris moped in silence.

As Willy lay in bed that night, his thoughts wandered. *Boy, I wonder what is in that room? Guess we'll have to find out some other time!*

THE END

If you're wondering with Willy, turn to page 79.

Or, turn to page 154.

"**H**ope you three are here to order something," said Betty, interrupting Sam's thoughts.

It didn't take anyone very long to decide what to order, and as they were all drinking their root beer floats, Chris reached in his pocket and unfolded the map.

"If this square is the church," Willy explained once more, "then I know that this line is the tunnel we already found."

"Why do you think this line in back of the church is another tunnel?" asked Chris.

"That's what we have to find out!" said Willy, slurping the last of his soda. "That part of the church hasn't been cleaned up yet," he added.

"Did you say 'clean up'? Oh, man, that reminds me—I have to go now," Sam said, standing up. "I told my dad I'd help him this afternoon. I'm glad you said something, Willy. You guys want to help clean out a garage that could pass for a disaster area?"

Chris and Willy didn't want to leave Sam out of the tunnel exploration, so they decided on an afternoon of hard labor. By supper time, they were sweaty, dirty, and tired.

When they said good night in front of Sam's house, Willy's last words were, "See you guys tomorrow morning on the church steps at sunup!"

64

CHOICE

Turn to page 33.

"Yes, Willy, before there were telephones, when there was a fire or someone was hurt or missing, the bell would be rung. Then everyone would run to the church to see how they could help."

"How did the people know there was danger and not just another meeting at church?" Willy asked.

"The bell was rung as fast as someone could pull the rope," said Mr. Whitehead. "But don't even practice that way of ringing a bell. It's better not to 'cry wolf,' you know."

Then he thanked them all for coming and asked them to be at church the following Sunday about thirty minutes before the service to take turns ringing the bell.

After they climbed down the ladder into the picture room, Jessica began asking Mr. Whitehead questions about one of the pictures. Willy and Sam hurried Chris down the staircase to the outside of the church. They excitedly showed him the map and began to make plans for the next day's exploring.

"Should we tell Mr. Whitehead?" asked Sam.

"Nah," said Willy. "We're not gonna mess with anything, we're just going to see if there really is another secret tunnel under the church."

"Too bad Jim and the others are going to miss this one," said Chris. Jim, another member of the Ringers and his sister, Tina, were on vacation in Chicago with their aunt and uncle. No one knew exactly when they would be coming back. Chris's cousin Jill had gone back to her parents for a few days. Pete was away at camp.

"Let's go to the Freeze and make plans," said Sam.

"Are you going to treat?" asked Chris, teasing his friend.

"Sure," Sam said nonchalantly, surprising them all. "My Aunt Stella just came to visit, and she always gives me five dollars."

"Sounds great to me," said Willy, heading toward the Common. "I'd really like to take another look at that map."

Moments later, Jessica came out of the church and walked slowly away by herself. She knew the boys, especially Willy, didn't want her with them. She hadn't wanted to move away from the city, but her dad had thought it would be a good idea for them to leave and spend some time in a small town. Jessica hadn't had very many friends, even in Washington, D.C., but she had had a good friend named Mandy. She missed her very much.

Then Jessica remembered the conversation she had just had with Mr. Whitehead and smiled. She loved listening to him talk about the way things were in the past. He had even told her that on Sunday afternoon she could look through some of the old books stacked on the shelves of the picture room. He wanted a list of the books that were there.

Not very many people would be happy about spending their summers going through some old books, Jessica realized, but she already knew she was different than many other kids. She loved to read about the way things used to be. She could hardly wait until next Sunday to ring the bell and maybe spend a peaceful afternoon poking around the picture room. Of course, she didn't know that peaceful was the last thing next Sunday would be!

CHOICE

If you want to go with Jessica next Sunday and ring the church bell, turn to page 104.

If you want to catch up with Willy and the other Ringers as they head toward the Freeze, turn to page 118.

"**I**'m getting sorta tired of stairs," Sam commented with a mischievous glint in his dark brown eyes. "Let's take the slide!"

"The slide?" asked Jessica.

"Yeah, the slide." Willy said nonchalantly as he headed toward the ladder to the attic. "C'mon, we'll show you."

"Maybe," Chris said thoughtfully, remembering the diary, "the slide is more than just a neat way to slide down through the building. Maybe the slaves used the slide to escape when the church was being searched. The letter seems to say that, doesn't it?"

"Good thought, Chris," Sam said as he started to climb the ladder to the attic. He immediately stuck his head back down through the hole and said, "But it doesn't mean we can't have a blast with it, does it?" The boys rushed up the ladder, and Jessica scrambled after them.

Moments later, they showed Jessica the dark hole beside the chimney in the attic floor. "What's down there?" she asked, trying not to sound afraid.

"There are steps built into the wall, Jess," Chris explained reassuringly, as he disappeared over the edge. "All you have to do is climb down. When the steps end, there's kind of a slide that goes into the basement."

Sam went down next, and then it was Jessica's turn.

She counted the rungs in the wall, tentatively reaching for each one with her foot. *Sixteen, seventeen, eighteen* . . . Then there was nothing but emptiness when she tried to find another rung.

"Let go, Jess," she could hear Chris's voice faintly below her in the darkness.

"Oh, c'mon," said Willy impatiently from above.

Gathering her courage, Jessica let go. Immediately she fell a short way and then slid down a tunnel made by the slick boards onto the floor of the church basement. Willy came out laughing right behind her. For some reason, he enjoyed the slide more than anyone.

"That was sort of fun," she admitted to Willy as they brushed themselves off. Sam and Chris were standing in a doorway at the end of the hallway that Jessica had never seen before. She knew instantly it was a secret panel.

"Hey, someone left the tunnel door open," Sam exclaimed.

"The outside door's open, too," Chris observed. They could see up the short set of stone steps that the secret door at the top was open about ten inches.

"Mr. Whitehead came in through the front door," Jessica pointed out.

"I'm not sure Mr. Whitehead even knows about this door, Jess," said Chris.

"Here's some mud on the carpet," Willy said, stooping down on one knee to touch the largest clump of mud. "And it's fresh."

Just then all four of them heard a scratching sound.

"It's coming from the back of the basement," Chris said.

"Let's go and see what it is," Sam said, as he started walking down the hall.

"But we don't know who it is," Jessica said hesitantly.

In unison the three boys turned around to give her a withering look.

"Of course we don't know who it is," explained Willy with exaggerated patience. "That's why we're investigating."

"I don't think its such a good idea," Jessica protested feebly.

CHOICE

Do they investigate? If they do, turn to page 113.

If they go up to Mr. Whitehead's study, turn to page 16.

Willy looked at the kitchen clock. It was only 7:00.

At 8:30, I'll call Chris and see if he's home yet, Willy decided, and settled down to wait. It was hard not to feel sorry for himself when the other boys were exploring a tunnel while he was stuck at home watching his sister.

A short time later, Carla came out of her room hugging Moses and said, "Hi, Willy. Where's Grandma?"

"She went to visit Great-Grandma Hattie," said Willy, reaching into the kitchen cabinet for Carla's favorite cereal. He felt like saying something mean to Carla, but he knew it wasn't her fault that he had to miss exploring the tunnel.

Exactly at 8:30, Willy called both Sam and Chris, but nobody was home. Impatiently, he sat down in front of the television with Carla to watch "Sesame Street." The day certainly wasn't turning out the way he had planned.

Just then, the phone rang. Willy wondered who could be calling at this hour. Carla answered it. She listened for a moment, then motioned him to come. The call was for him.

72

CHOICE ⇒

Funny thing about phone calls, you never know who it is
until you answer. If this call is from Chris, turn to page
120.

If the call is from someone else, turn to page 94.

Chris could tell his friends were just as upset as he was at being so clearly surprised by a girl. He shrugged his shoulders and said, "No place special."

"I'm ready for another of those great Ringer adventures," said Jill. "So, what shall we do?"

"Oh, nothing," said Willy with just a touch of sullenness in his voice.

Jill noticed it. "Oh, I get it," she said. "You guys are mad at me because I surprised you, right?" She looked at the three boys standing there who wouldn't look back at her. She *was* right. There were some heavy moments of silence. Jill thought about the times they had played pranks on her. Most of the time she had tried to be a good sport. She wanted these guys to be her friends. They had already had a lot of fun together. Maybe she needed to apologize for surprising them.

But the silence had been more than the boys could bear. They *knew* better. They glanced at each other guiltily. Finally Chris said, "You're right, I think we were ticked that you played such a neat trick on us. I guess we're used to being on the giving instead of the getting end of surprises." Both Sam and Willy nodded in agreement.

Sam said, "Actually, Jill, we did have some plans for this afternoon. Want to come along?"

74

 **CHOICE**

Turn to page 143.

The three boys ran all the way to the church. The front door was locked.

"I say it's time to go in the secret side entrance, guys," Willy decided. Since the church was open most of the time, the Ringers hadn't had to use that way in very often.

Both Chris and Sam thought that was a good idea. When they got around to that door, though, they discovered it was jammed, like someone had wedged it shut from behind to lock it.

"What good is finding a map," asked Willy, "if you get locked out of the place you're trying to explore?"

"Let's go over to the abandoned field behind the church and hide in the grass. These tunnels have to come out somewhere. Maybe we can find the other end of one of them. And while we're looking, we can pretend we're traveling on the Underground Railroad that Great-Grandma Hattie told us about!" suggested Sam.

Chris looked at Sam condescendingly. "Aren't we a little old to play pretend?"

Sam only shrugged.

"C'mon, Chris," Willy urged. "We don't have anything better to do until we can get into the church and check out the old map."

"If it even is a map," Chris muttered.

The three boys wandered over to the field and waded

through the waist-high grass. Sam tested the lowest limb of the huge old maple tree that stood alone out in the field, and then swung himself up and began to climb.

Willy found a sturdy stick that was shaped in a *V* and pulled off his stretch belt. He tied one end of his belt to each of the ends of the *V* and created a makeshift slingshot. He found some pebbles and began to shoot at imaginary enemies hiding in the tall grass.

Chris just picked up a large branch and began to absently swish it through the grass as he walked up the little hill.

Now if Sam hadn't been looking down from nearly the top of the tree at the exact spot where Chris was swishing his stick, he might have never seen it. Chris didn't even see it, and he was right on top of it. But there is something about a view from a tree that lets you see things that you sometimes miss when you're on the ground.

"Hey, Chris," Sam called down. "Stand still!"

Chris stopped and looked up at Sam skeptically. "What is it?"

"Look down, beside that bush."

"I don't see anything."

"Look again!"

This time Chris saw what Sam meant. "Oh, wow! Willy, come here quick!"

It was a wooden door set into the side of the small hill!

Sam scrambled down the tree, and the three of them tore the grass and moss away from the opening. The door almost fell apart when they opened it. Behind it was the beginning of a tunnel in the direction of the church. Too excited for words, the boys looked at each other for a moment.

"Anybody have a flashlight?" Chris asked half teasingly.

"I do," said Sam quietly, pulling a large, ugly pen out of his pocket. The pen had *James Dry Cleaning* written across one side in pink letters.

"That's one ugly pen," said Chris skeptically.

"It also has a flashlight at one end," Sam explained. "My Aunt Stella and Uncle Morris are visiting us this week. Uncle Morris gave me this just before I was leaving today. I had to thank him, even if it is ugly. I didn't want to hurt his feelings, so I told him I'd take it with me and show my friends."

"And you have," remarked Willy. "Lead the way, Sam."

Sam crawled into the tunnel. Willy and Chris followed. Within a few yards, the tunnel got high enough that they could almost stand up. Before long, the shaft began to slope downward and become narrower. At last, Sam's little flashlight beam showed only solid earth in front of them.

"It's a dead end," Chris said unhappily.

Then Willy, who had been silent for a few moments, suddenly hissed, "Look up!"

All three boys looked up and there, in the ceiling of the tunnel, was another door! It was almost out of their reach, but by standing on Chris and Sam's hands and pushing against it, Willy managed to open the door a crack. He couldn't see beyond the opening in the darkness. But he could tell something heavy was on the door.

"I guess we'll have to turn back," said Sam regretfully. The three boys retraced their steps until they were in the abandoned field once more.

"The map!" cried Willy suddenly. "Hey, Chris, do you have the map?"

Chris pulled it out of his jeans pocket and smoothed it out.

"Look!" exclaimed Willy. "I think we discovered the back entrance to the secret tunnel! See where that one line keeps going? Well, I think we just found out why! Now we just need to find out how we can get from the church to that ceiling door we found."

"You may be right," admitted Chris. "At least we finally got to do some exploring!"

"Ya know, I'm really thirsty!" exclaimed Willy. "Let's all go over to the Freeze and get a soda before we go home!"

"Maybe tomorrow we can get into the church and look for the other entrance," Chris added. *Now that was something to look forward to,* he thought.

THE END

Turn to page 154.

Sam and Willy reluctantly agreed to try Chris's plan.
They all went back out into the hallway, and Chris chose
the farthest door from the secret basement door for them to
check. That room seemed a little larger than the first one
they had visited. But the smells were the same. The new
room had been panelled with vertical wood strips called
wainscoting. Large flakes of paint were peeling off.

Chris's heart beat a little faster. He said, "Some of
these strips may be loose so that they slide over as a
hidden doorway." The boys each started on a wall. Willy,
who chose the wall opposite the door, started on the left
side of the wall and worked to his right. He pushed back
and forth on the wood paneling, but nothing budged. He
could tell from the grunts behind him that Sam and Chris
were having the same problem. By the time he got to the
right side of his wall, he was more than ready to quit. He
gave the last section a shove, expecting to push himself
away and head for the door. Instead, the entire wall swung
away from him.

"Hey! What's this?" Willy yelled with instant
excitement. Chris and Sam were beside him in a flash.
Chris picked up the candle that Willy had set in the middle
of the floor and lifted it high. The light revealed the
entrance to a tunnel!

The three boys crawled into the tunnel; the ceiling

was only about three feet high. The passageway bent around to the left and went directly away from the church. They also found themselves crawling slightly downhill. This tunnel had the same heavy timbers that braced the walls in the first tunnel they had found.

After a few moments, Chris whispered, "Well, Willy, I guess we *did* find a map!"

They hadn't gone too far when the tunnel opened up into a small room. There were solid planks making up all the walls. Their entrance looked like the only way into the room. There was a wooden box with a cover against the far wall.

Sam wandered over to the left and, when he looked back at the entrance they had just used, asked Willy to hold the candle in his direction. Hanging on the wall was a board with some words painted on it. The three boys gathered around to figure out what was written.

Willy slowly read, "Dedicated to God's service in memory of our white brothers and colored brother who died in the cave-in, Jim B., Aaron S., and Joshua W." He stopped, then thought out loud, "I wonder when all this happened?"

Chris wandered over to the wooden crate and lifted the top. Several moths flew out and made him jump a little. "Hey, look at this!" said Willy as he reached into the box and began to rummage through what looked like a pile of blankets. "There's some old clothes in here." He picked up an old blue coat and held it up. The fabric was rotting in places and looked as if it had been patched.

"Check the pockets," Sam suggested.

Willy put his hand in one of the pockets and pulled out a piece of old paper.

"Is it a newspaper?" asked Chris.

"No," said Willy, as he smoothed out the paper. "It looks like a wanted poster!"

The three boys stared at the old paper. At the top were the words, "$250.00 Reward in Cash Money for the return of ———— following ———— slaves ————"

"Slaves!" cried Willy. "This is really old!"

Then the printing faded, and they couldn't make out very many of the words, but it looked like a list of names.

"I think that word says *Ezra*," said Sam.

"Maybe this word's *Joshua*," Willy added.

"Wait a minute, guys," said Chris looking at the poster and the pile of blankets, "Do you know what we found?"

"Yes," said Willy excitedly, remembering his Great-Grandma Hattie's stories. "This church must have had something to do with the Underground Railroad! So that's what all these tunnels and secrets are about! I can't wait to tell Great-Grandma Hattie and to show her this poster!"

Willy carefully refolded the poster and turned to go home.

"Just a minute, Willy," Chris said thoughtfully. "I'll bet that if someone was hiding slaves in this room, then there must be another way out."

"What?" said Willy.

"Well, just suppose the slaves were in this room, and the slave catchers were searching the church. If there was

82

another way out, someone else could come and sneak the slaves away through another door."

"I don't see any other doors," said Sam.

"Neither do I," said Willy, "Let's go back now. We can always come back tomorrow. I can't wait to show this poster to Great-Grandma Hattie!"

Once he'd thought of it, Chris knew he'd be back to look for a way out of this room. He did have to agree from the way the walls were built that there didn't seem to be any place for a door. *But that,* he thought, *is what makes all this so interesting!*

As they turned to leave, they couldn't help but notice the sign on the wall once more. Sam whistled softly. "Whatever went on around here was really serious. People died digging these tunnels. I hope it was worth it."

Willy smiled and said, "If this was part of the Underground Railroad, then it was worth it!"

THE END

Turn to page 154.

"The Underground Railroad?" Mr. Whitehead exclaimed, as Willy handed him the diary. "Well, I've heard of the Railroad running through Washington, but could this church have been one of the stations? Let's see that letter you found, Sam."

Sam handed over the letter that had fallen out of the poetry book.

Mr. Whitehead leaned back in his chair as he read the short note. "Hmmm, 'Keep thee safe.' The note was probably written by Quakers." He looked up a moment and smiled at the Ringers clustered around his desk. "You remind me of me fifty years ago," he chuckled. "So curious! Well, you're making some of the same discoveries I made as a child. I spent countless hours praying and playing in this church. They changed my life, as I hope they will change yours. I'll help you along the way, but I think you should work a lot of things out on your own. This is your adventure. I hope you realize how big a part God had in it!"

Willy shrugged and asked the question that was on everybody's mind, "What are Quakers?"

Mr. Whitehead thought for a moment, then answered, "Quakers are a very serious group of Christians who try to be as obedient as possible to what the Bible teaches. They were given that name years ago because many of them would kind of tremble in fear and reverence during their meetings. Now that you mention it, I do remember my parents talking about Quakers in this church . . ."

He paused, then continued, "The Quakers were one of the most outspoken and active groups against slavery in our country. A number of them worked very hard to free the slaves."

Willy nodded, remembering the picture of "Uncle Louis" in the picture room.

"Now, you all know what *baggage* and *passengers* mean, don't you?"

"The escaped slaves," Jessica said softly.

Mr. Whitehead nodded. "And what was a *conductor?*"

"Someone who took the slaves to the next station," Willy said decisively. "My Great-Grandma Hattie knows a lot about the Underground Railroad. Her grandfather was a passenger!"

"Perhaps she would agree to tell us all some stories about the Railroad," Mr. Whitehead suggested. "I hope you plan to show her what you have found."

"We sure do!" declared Willy.

"The Leonard Grimes in this note was probably a conductor," Chris guessed, reading the note once more.

"You may be right, Chris," Mr. Whitehead agreed. "This is really quite a treasure! I'm sure that some of the history professors at the university will be very excited to see what you have found."

"Alright! Let's celebrate!" said Sam exuberantly, throwing his arms up in the air.

"A celebration is an excellent idea!" agreed Mr.

Whitehead. "How about if I treat everyone to their favorite at the Freeze?"

All the Ringers quickly agreed!

"I knew this old church would have more secrets to share," Willy said happily, as the Ringers walked with Mr. Whitehead across the Common to the Freeze.

Later that week Jessica couldn't resist going to the library (of course) and looking up the name Leonard Grimes. This is what she found:

Leonard Grimes was a black man born of free parents, and never was himself a slave. Nevertheless, he was a resourceful conductor of the Underground Railroad in Washington, D.C. Using his own money, he purchased a number of horses and carriages, which he used for the Railroad.

Once while transporting a family through Virginia, he was arrested and sentenced to two years in prison at Richmond, Virginia. When he was released, he moved to Boston and became the pastor of the Twelfth Street Baptist Church, where he established a major station on the Underground Railroad. On several occasions, he and his congregation purchased the freedom of individual slaves.

Jessica realized the Ringers had only begun to uncover the story of the Underground Railroad station in Millersburg.

86

THE END

Turn to page 154.

Quickly Jessica raced out of the church and ran to Mr. Whitehead's house.

"I think someone's in the church attic because I heard a very loud crash, and then it sounded like someone was calling for help and . . ."

"Let's go, Jess," the old man said, reaching for his car keys. "You can tell me the rest of the story on the way over to the church."

They entered the church, and just as they were about to climb the staircase, Jessica thought that Mr. Whitehead did a very strange thing. He closed his eyes and simply said, "Take care of us, Lord; we are your people."

And the sheep of your pasture. The words from the Bible verse sprung into Jessica's mind.

"I want you to stay here," Mr. Whitehead said firmly to Jessica. "We don't know who's up there."

Jessica waited for several long moments as she heard Mr. Whitehead's footsteps above her in the picture room. She wished that she knew how to pray, because if she did, she would be asking God to take care of Pastor Leonard!

"Jess, come up here!" Pastor Leonard called urgently.

She bounded up the stairs and saw Willy sitting on the floor. He looked kind of dazed.

"Is he OK?" she asked.

"I think his leg is broken." Pastor Leonard looked very

worried. "I want you to stay with him while I get help," he added as he went down the stairs.

Jessica looked at Willy. He had lain back down on the floor and had thrown his arm over his face. Jessica sat on the floor beside him. She felt very helpless. She knew that Willy was in a lot of pain, but she didn't know what to do.

Maybe if I just start talking, she thought, *Willy won't think about his leg hurting so much.*

So Jessica began to tell Willy some of her favorite stories from the history books she had read. Willy groaned. Jessica couldn't tell if it was because his leg hurt or because he hated history.

She knew that most boys liked war stories, so she tried to remember some war stories to tell him. She started telling stories about the Civil War, and then she was telling him about the diary and the Underground Railroad. Willy didn't move, but he didn't tell her to be quiet either, so Jessica just kept talking.

Finally she heard Pastor Leonard's voice below.

"Help's here, Willy!" she whispered gratefully, as two men in white uniforms with a stretcher between them came up the staircase.

Willy had broken his leg and had to be on crutches for almost two months. Eventually, he learned to do several tricks with his crutches and still managed to go on several adventures, even with his leg in a cast.

But he did have more free time and actually spent some time reading books, even books about history, especially the Civil War. And amazingly enough, the person who cheered him up the most was Jessica!

THE END

Turn to page 154.

"**N**o, that's OK, you go ahead," Jessica said without looking at Chris. She knew he had only asked her because he was trying to be polite. Just two nights ago, when Mrs. Martin had invited her father and her over for a visit, Jessica had overheard Mrs. Martin tell her father that Chris would "be sure to invite Jessica to some of his activities."

"Well, OK," said Chris. "Good-bye, Mrs. Whitehead," he called as he turned to catch up with the other boys.

Jessica picked up her purse and started to leave.

"Good-bye, Jessica," Mrs. Whitehead said softly.

"G'bye," Jessica mumbled as she left the Sunday school room.

She didn't even look at the carvings of the lion and the lamb that she had to pass by at the top of the basement stairs. She kept her head down as she was leaving the church.

"Jessica! Just the person I was looking for!" Jessica looked up and saw Mr. Whitehead coming toward her. "Why don't you come home and have some lunch with Mrs. Whitehead and me? You can call your dad from our house to let him know, but I'm sure it will be OK. I spoke with him earlier." He seemed to remember something else, "Oh, and after lunch, perhaps you might like to come back to the church with me. While I study for a little while, you might want to do some exploring in the picture room."

Jessica almost said no even though she had been hoping for a chance to read some of the old books in the picture room. But Mr. Whitehead really seemed to want her to come. *His eyes are kind,* she noticed. *Just like my grandfather's.* She decided to have lunch with the Whiteheads.

After lunch, Mr. Whitehead was as good as his word. He walked with her to the old church. He told her to enjoy herself looking through the old books in the picture room. He said he would be in his office if she needed anything. She was reaching for the lamb's ear as he walked away.

Jessica climbed the staircase to the picture room and knelt down by the bookcase. The old books had the satisfyingly musty smell of old things. Jessica settled down to a completely delightful time. An old rag helped wipe the dust off as she removed each book from the shelf. She pored through some collections of poems and glanced through a few old school books. There were several old family Bibles. It was among these that she found a book that had been written by hand. Page after page was filled with small, beautiful writing. The dates at the top of each page caught her attention. This was a diary!

Eagerly she turned to the beginning of the book and began to read. The writer of the diary began by describing her wedding in Boston. Then she described traveling with her husband after he was called to pastor the church at Millersburg. Jessica lost track of time as she read how difficult it was for the young woman to make friends in the new town.

June 18, 1851
How much I miss Boston and all of the

*wonderful friends that I had to leave behind!
This town seems so strange to me! And I must
seem rather "strange" to them, with my
different speech and my city ways.*

Just like me, Jessica thought, and continued to read.
Then came a series of entries that referred to something
else that was happening in the church.

> *Oct 8, 1851*
>
> *Picked up three large packages and two
> small ones. All were very cold. Used up all the
> old clothing. Have to ask ladies in sewing
> group for some more, especially warm coats.*
>
> *Oct 22, 1851*
>
> *John got back today very late from the next
> station. Fortunately we have heard that Ezra
> and Joshua were delivered safely to freedom!
> Praise be to God and to our brother Thomas
> Garrett!*
>
> *Oct 25, 1851*
>
> *Sunday services. How sad to not be able to
> worship together. We are all his people, the
> sheep of his pasture.*

That's part of our Bible verse, Jessica thought, as she
continued to read.

> *Oct 30, 1851*
>
> *Stored eleven packages. Slave catchers
> searched the church and found nothing. This
> new law has made criminals of us all!*

Gradually, Jessica began to understand what she was
reading. The woman writing the diary was helping slaves

escape! That idea filled her with a strange sense of fear and excitement. It was like she was looking over the shoulder of someone from the past who was doing something very dangerous because it was right. She wondered if this woman had been part of the Underground Railroad that she had learned about in her American history class. She would have to check to see if the dates matched.

"Jessica, are you ready to leave now?" Jessica heard Mr. Whitehead's voice call from downstairs.

"I'll be right there," she said as she stood up and brushed the dust off her skirt. Quickly she put the diary in her purse. It didn't occur to her that it might be wrong to take something out of the church that wasn't hers. She climbed down the staircase and joined Mr. Whitehead, who walked her home.

When she got home, she went to her room, locked the door, and began to read the diary. It got more and more exciting with each new page! Jessica realized that there must have been several secret rooms in the church that were being used to hide the slaves!

Chris would really think this was neat! Jessica thought. But why should she tell him about the diary? After all, none of the boys had bothered to include her in their adventures.

CHOICE ⇒

If she tells the boys about the diary, turn to page 59.

If she explores the church on her own, turn to page 122.

"Willy, it's Grandma," Carla said. "She says that after lunch, she's bringing Great-Grandma Hattie over here for a visit."

"Hey, that's great!" Willy exclaimed. "Maybe this afternoon I'll be able to explore the tunnel with the guys after all!"

The day was definitely taking a turn for the better, Willy decided. He was so happy that, after "Sesame Street" was over, he even played Go Fish with Carla. Go Fish was her favorite game, but Willy thought it was pretty stupid. Just as he started to make sandwiches for lunch, the front door opened and in walked Grandma and Great-Grandma Hattie!

Great-Grandma Hattie was the oldest person that Willy knew. She was born before people had cars or electricity. She often told stories about the way things were when she was growing up on a farm with ten brothers and sisters. Willy loved to listen to Great-Grandma Hattie's stories, even if she sometimes forgot and told him the same story a couple of times.

After hugs and kisses all around, Willy's grandma went into the kitchen to make some phone calls. Great-Grandma Hattie settled into a chair, and Carla climbed into her lap.

"Now, then," said Great-Grandma Hattie, "How have you children been?"

"Fine, Great-Grandma," said Carla, "and could you please tell us a story?"

"Yes, indeed, I'll be glad to tell you one of my stories. What story would you like?"

"Tell us the one about how you got your name," said Carla.

Willy flopped onto the floor and got comfortable. He decided to wait a couple of minutes before he tried to find Chris and Sam. This story was one of his favorites too.

Just then, the doorbell rang. Willy got up and opened the door. There stood Sam and Chris!

"Hey, Willy, where were you this morning?"

"I had to watch Carla. But my grandma's here now." Willy stepped out on the porch. "Did you guys find any secret tunnels?"

"No, we were tempted, but we decided to wait for you," Chris said.

Just then Carla came out onto the porch. "Willy, Great-Grandma Hattie's waiting to tell us her story. She says your friends are welcome to listen too."

Willy wanted to do both things at once—listen to Great-Grandma Hattie's story and look for the secret tunnel. He wasn't sure how Sam and Chris would feel about sticking around. They had a choice to make.

96

CHOICE ⇒

If they listen to Great-Grandma Hattie's story, turn to page 13.

If they go and look for the tunnel, turn to page 75.

"**S**o, let's say this *is* a map," Willy explained. "I think the largest square is the church, and this squiggly line to the left is that old dirt passageway we found down the second flight of stairs."

"But what about this funny line going out from the back of the church?" Sam asked. "It looks like a snake that swallowed a mouse."

"That's got to be another tunnel!" declared Willy. "And I think we should explore it!"

"OK by me," said Sam, looking at the map once more.

"Hello, boys!" Leonard Whitehead's deep voice startled the two boys. Sam quickly folded up the map and put it in his pocket. They turned around to see Mr. Whitehead climbing up the secret staircase, followed closely by Chris and Jessica.

Willy made a face when he saw Jessica that Chris couldn't help but notice. He didn't think his friend was giving Jessica much of a chance. He had also noticed that Sam had stuffed something quickly in his pocket as they entered the room.

"So this is where the secret stairway leads," Jessica said softly, staring wide-eyed around the picture room. She loved old things!

Jessica was one of those people who seemed to do everything quietly, as if she was afraid someone might really see her. Sometimes she acted shy. Actually, Jessica was so sure she wasn't pretty or very interesting that she just tried to attract as little attention as possible.

"Jess," said Pastor Leonard, "this picture room is only the first place the secret passage leads. There's even more to be discovered. But for now, I think we're ready to make you a new Ringer. Shall we go up?"

Everyone nodded. Willy's nod had a slight negative slant to it. Jessica had already seen that near the center of the room was a ladder leading up to an opening in the ceiling. Next to the ladder hung a rope. Willy was the first one to scamper up the ladder to the attic. The others followed. Once they were all in the attic, Jess's curiosity got the best of her.

"Why are we coming up here to ring the bell when the rope goes all the way down to that room?" she asked.

"Sometimes we do use the rope below," answered Chris. "But the sound effects up here are awesome!" Then he added, "There's even another rope that can be used from the balcony of the church. I guess that's the official rope. We like this secret one better."

"Yeah," added Sam with a chuckle. "And you really can't be a Ringer till you've heard this bell up close. After that it's a wonder you can hear anything at all!"

Mr. Whitehead got their attention and gave a few instructions to Jessica. "To ring this bell, stand with your weight over both feet and grasp the rope above your head, then pull down hard. This church bell is a very old one, forged before the Civil War, and it's quite heavy."

Mr. Whitehead gave a long, smooth pull on the rope. Everyone looked up.

Bong, bong, bong!

The deep sounds fell on them like thunder. Jessica shivered and closed her eyes as the floor under her feet vibrated. It was loud and wonderful. She had never heard and felt sound at the same time with such intensity.

"OK, Jessica, now you try." Mr. Whitehead handed her the rope as the echo died away. She grasped it and tugged. The bell gave one feeble clink. Willy snickered, but fortunately Jessica didn't hear him. She was concentrating instead on what her kind new friend was saying. After several tries, she managed to give the bell a firm ring.

"That's it," said Sam encouragingly. "You'll get the *hang* of it in no time." He made sure no one missed the pun. Jess smiled her thanks.

Willy was next. He pulled as hard as he could, and the bell rang very loudly. Then Sam and finally Chris took a turn.

"Excellent!" said Mr. Whitehead approvingly. "When you ring the bell to call people for church, I want you to count, one-rest, two-rest, three-rest. Go ahead, I want each of you to try."

After everyone had taken another turn, Jess asked a question. "When was the bell rung in the old days?"

Mr. Whitehead told them a little about the history of the church bell. Willy let his mind wander, but Jessica listened to every word. She loved history.

"Bells were used to call people for church on Sundays and for midweek prayer meeting." *Wouldn't it be nice to start a midweek prayer meeting?* Mr. Whitehead added to

100

himself. "And of course the bell was always rung if there was danger."

"Danger?" asked Willy. That word always got his attention.

Turn to page 65.

It was late afternoon when Chris and Jill turned onto Maple Street and walked into city hall. The directory told them the police station was in the basement. Millersburg didn't need a very large police force. There were hardly ever more than two policemen on duty at once.

The policeman at the front desk looked up as he heard the door open and smiled when he saw Chris. Chris recognized his old baseball coach, Officer Gary.

"Hi, Chris, been playing much baseball lately?" Officer Gary quirked an eyebrow as he saw Jill and smiled as if he and Chris shared a secret. Chris hated the way adults did that when they saw him with a girl! Hastily he introduced his cousin to Officer Gary.

"OK, what brings you two to the police station?" Officer Gary asked, getting down to business and pulling out a notepad from the desk drawer.

"We've seen some pretty strange things," Chris began. He then proceeded to tell Officer Gary what had happened.

Officer Gary listened gravely to Chris's story and wrote down exactly what Chris said on the notepad. He whistled softly when Jill handed him the panel from the milk carton.

"You're sure this is who he looks like?" he asked. Chris nodded.

"OK. The first thing to do will be to call the missing

kids hotline," said Officer Gary as he picked up the phone. He spoke for a few minutes to someone and then turned back to Jill and Chris. His look was serious. "The boy on this picture was taken from a school playground in Baltimore a month ago. The amazing thing is that his picture just got on the milk cartons. But the people at the missing kids center say this Trent Gallagher has been found."

Chris and Jill were very disappointed. Frustrated, too. Officer Gary noticed their frowns and said, "Listen, kids, I appreciate that you took time to check out your suspicions. If more people did that, more kids would be found. But it just doesn't look like this is a kidnapping case. Maybe you just spotted this kid after he did something wrong. He looked scared because he was on the way to get punished." He smiled and picked up some papers from his desk. Chris and Jill took the hint that the conversation was over.

They thanked Officer Gary and left the police station.

"Do you think he believed us?" Jill asked Chris as they crossed Maple Street and walked down Main Street to the old church.

"I think so," Chris thought out loud. "Otherwise he wouldn't have made that call. But I still think there's something wrong going on here. I guess it's up to us to find out what it is."

When they got back to the factory, Willy and Sam were anxious. "Where are the cops?" asked Willy.

"They're not coming," answered Jill.

"This kid Trent was found just a few days ago. So the

one we saw can't be the one on the milk carton," added Chris. "But I'm still not sure about what's going on here," he continued, nodding toward the apartment.

Sam tried to be helpful. "Maybe we were all letting our imaginations run away with us! I think we should forget this wild goose chase. After all, we did find that map yesterday, and we haven't even had a chance to check it out!"

"What map?" asked Jill.

"Oh, nothing, just a piece of paper with squiggles on it," said Willy, smirking at Chris.

Chris wasn't listening. He was making up his mind to do something. "Look, you guys, I think this is serious," he said. "I'm not ready to quit. We have a possible kidnapping here. Let's meet right here tomorrow morning first thing and see what we can do!"

The others looked at each other trying to decide what they should do.

CHOICE ⇒

If they decide that Trent Gallagher was kidnapped, turn to page 117.

If they decide that it's time to check out the map, turn to page 33.

"**S**hout for joy to the Lord, all the earth . . ." Jessica muttered the words quietly under her breath on her way to Sunday school. She shuffled along, checking the crumpled paper in her hand over and over. Memorizing was hard! She wasn't familiar with the Bible, so the ideas were new and strange to her. But Mrs. Whitehead, their Sunday school teacher, had given them a Bible verse to learn every Sunday. All the other kids learned the verses, even the boys. Jessica didn't want to look stupid, so she learned the verses too.

"The Lord is God, it is he who made us . . ." Jessica brushed her long hair out of her eyes and scrunched her shoulders down to make herself look shorter because she saw the boys up ahead. She still couldn't believe that she was going to church every Sunday, especially in the summer when it felt *sooo* great to be able to sleep in. And now, because of Mr. Whitehead, she had to get up even earlier to ring the stupid old bell.

But even as she thought about the bell, Jessica started to get excited. She didn't really think ringing the bell was stupid. She was glad she had tagged along behind Chris when the boys were exploring the old church because Mr. Whitehead had asked her to ring the bell too. So she secretly pretended that she was part of the gang, the Ringers, even though she knew that the boys would probably never let her go on any adventures with them.

Then she took a deep breath and started the whole verse over again. "Shout for joy . . ." She didn't pay any attention to the words, she just said them as fast as she could, "We are his people, the sheep of his pasture."

Whew! I'm glad that's over, she thought as she came to the front of the church. The big wooden doors stood before her with their carvings of the lion and the lamb. Jessica put her hand on the lamb's ear and tugged. She was thankful that Mr. Whitehead had showed her how to open the door to the secret staircase. The door swung open, and she climbed the stairs to the picture room. Above her in the attic she could hear the boys' voices and the deeper voice of Mr. Whitehead.

"Where's Jessica?" she heard him ask.

"Aw, I don't know. Probably sneaking around somewhere, spying on us."

"Willy!" said Mr. Whitehead with a disappointed tone in his voice.

"I'm sure she's coming," Chris said. But he didn't sound very enthusiastic about it.

Just as she was about to climb the ladder to the attic, Jessica froze for a moment. It really hurt to know that the boys didn't want her around. Maybe she shouldn't ring the bell with them after all but quietly go back down the staircase and make up an excuse or something to explain why she didn't show up.

106

CHOICE ⇛

If she rings the bell, turn to page 45.

If she hides, turn to page 9.

Willy inched his way down the long stairway to the earth tunnel. By the time he reached the bottom he could definitely hear voices in the tunnel! *Now would be a good time to pray,* he thought. He remembered what Mrs. Whitehead had said about praying: "You don't need to use big words to talk to God. When you pray, just thank him for everything he's given you and humbly tell him what you need."

Willy knew what he needed. He was pretty sure God knew it too, but he whispered to God anyway, "Dear God, I'm really scared. Please help me to get out of here. Oh, and please keep Carla safe," he added guiltily. Willy didn't bother to close his eyes because the tunnel was pitch black!

Taking a deep breath, Willy began moving along the tunnel. He could hear voices far away. His heart kept beating faster. After turning two corners, he suddenly saw the beam of a flashlight casting eerie shadows on the wall. His knees wanted to buckle. The shadows were coming toward him! Willy was so frightened he couldn't move for a moment. The flashlight beam shone right in his eyes!

For some reason, the light made him move. Willy spun away from the light in complete fear and bumped his way back along the tunnel. He tripped up the stairs and came to a stop at the door. There was no place to go.

"Help, somebody help me!" he screamed at the top of his lungs, pounding on the basement door.

"Willy?"

Willy turned and looked down into the tunnel. The voice was familiar. He sagged against the doorway in relief as he realized Mr. Whitehead was standing at the bottom of the stairs.

"Mr. Whitehead! I thought you were a burglar or something!"

The old man laughed. "Hardly a burglar, Willy. You gave us quite a surprise, too. Come down here for a moment. I want to introduce you to someone."

Willy looked beyond Pastor Leonard and saw a slender woman with silver glasses holding up a lamp. He stepped down toward them.

"Willy, this is Alice Turner. Mrs. Turner is doing some research in this area for a book she is writing on the Underground Railroad. Alice, Willy is one of the Ringers I was telling you about."

"The Underground Railroad," exclaimed Willy, "I know a little about that! My great-great-great-grandfather was a passenger!"

"So was my great-great-grandfather," said Mrs. Turner. "He used to tell me some wonderful stories."

"Mrs. Turner thinks that this church actually might have been a station on the railroad. She's going to be doing some investigating here for the next couple days." Pastor Leonard added, with a gleam in his eyes, "I told her you boys were experts in exploring and might want to help her."

Willy thought about the map that he had found and said, "I think we might be able to help."

"I'd really appreciate it, Willy," Mrs. Turner added.

"And, ah, Mr. Whitehead, do you know how to open this door?" Willy asked. "I shut it by accident, and I really need to get home right away."

"Sure, Willy," said Mr. Whitehead, showing him the secret latch that released the door. Willy tried to move quickly but graciously out of the tunnel.

"It was nice to meet you, Mrs. Turner," Willy called over his shoulder. "I'll see you later."

"Good-bye, Willy," Mrs. Turner replied. "I'm looking forward to seeing you again. Bring your friends by later."

Willy raced back to his home. When he got there, he tiptoed upstairs to Carla's bedroom. She was still asleep! *Amazing!* he thought, *She slept right through "Sesame Street"!*

Willy went downstairs, flopped down in his father's recliner and closed his eyes for a moment. There was something important he still had to do.

"Thank you, God," Willy said, "for keeping Carla and me safe! I'll sure try to think a lot more before I do things in the future."

THE END

Turn to page 154.

Right after a quick lunch, the boys headed back to the church.

On the way, Sam said, "So, Willy, what's the plan now? You're sure someone's in the main tunnel. We'll sneak up on him, subdue him with some nifty karate moves, tie him up, and call the police, right? Maybe we should stop by my house so I can change into my ninja outfit."

Not to be outdone, Willy smirked and said, "You mean that costume you got from cereal box tops?"

Sam yelled, "Yee, yaa!" at the top of his lungs and began to chase Willy in circles. He made exaggerated cutting motions with his hands.

Willy grabbed Chris to use him as a shield. "Save me from those lethal weapons!" he shouted.

Chris allowed himself to be helplessly pushed back and forth between his friends for a few moments. But he decided it was time to become actively involved. After shouting several martial arts yells and making some motions with his hands, he faced his friends. "You may think I am just a hopeless victim, my honorable enemies. But I have a secret weapon! You know karate—but I know kawasaki!"

His announcement got the reaction he hoped. Sam and Willy looked at each other and mouthed the word

Chris had just used. Both of them began to laugh uncontrollably. They tried to keep the battle going, but it was hard to do martial arts amid fits of laughter. They had to admit they were no match for Chris's secret skill. A truce was declared.

"You usually aren't that funny," said Sam, "but I have to tell you that was pretty good, Chris."

Chris was pleased. He thought how great it was to have good friends. He also thought how strange it was that he had made them laugh. He wasn't trying to be funny, he was just joining the fight. What he had said was the first thing that came to mind. He was glad it turned out to be a good joke.

As the boys turned the corner onto Main Street, Sam glanced back for an instant. Almost immediately, he grabbed the others and shoved them against the brick wall of the antique store. "Quiet!" he hissed. "Somebody's following us."

Willy said, "What are we waiting for? Let's get out of here!"

Chris said, "No, let's see who it is."

"What are we going to do?" whispered Willy sarcastically. "Jump out and kawasaki them to death?"

Sam began to snicker again.

112

CHOICE ⟹

If the boys try to find out who's following them, turn to page 134.

If the boys run, turn to page 152.

Jessica hung back in the hall while Willy, Chris, and Sam followed the mud trail to a large closet in the back of the church basement. The door was partly open. The three boys halted in the hall right in front of the closet.

"Boy, it's sure dark in there," whispered Willy. "I wonder if there's a light switch."

"What do you think is in there?" asked Sam.

Jessica hesitantly inched down the corridor until she was about six feet behind the boys.

"There's some candles and some matches in the closet in Mrs. Whitehead's Sunday school room," she volunteered. At the sound of her voice, a frantic scratching noise came from the closet.

Sam and Chris ran quickly to get the candles. Moments later the four of them looked like a scary group of carolers, each holding a flickering candle.

"You first, Willy," Sam said, gesturing at him with his wax baton.

"Why me?" said Willy indignantly.

"Because you're the bravest," Sam said solemnly.

Willy took the candle and walked into the closet. The scratching noise stopped and was replaced with a soft whimper.

"Hey, guys," Willy called softly, "come in here, will ya?"

Cautiously, Jessica, Chris, and Sam edged into the closet. There, on a pile of old rags, was a large gray shaggy dog!

"Boy, does he smell!" Sam said disapprovingly.

"He's pretty dirty," Chris added.

"He likes me," said Willy, as the dog slurped its huge tongue over his hand. "I guess he decided this church was a pretty safe place to hide!"

"I'd sure like to know how he managed to find and open both the doors to get in here," Chris wondered out loud.

"I guess he's as smart as he is beautiful!" said Jessica gently as she dropped down on the floor and reached out her hand timidly toward the dog. The dog slurped her hand as well. Jessica gingerly patted the dog's side. "He really does need a bath," she admitted.

"What'll we do with him?" asked Sam.

"I can't take him home," said Chris. "Gracie, our basset hound, would be jealous if I got another dog."

"I'd love to take him home," said Sam sadly, "but our landlord always says 'no pets!'"

"My mom likes cats," Willy said glumly. "We have three. But I'd much rather have a dog."

"I'll take him home," Jessica declared, jumping up. "I'm sure my dad will let me keep him! At least till we find out who he belongs to. One thing's for sure, we can't leave him here."

"The Freeze has a phone. You can call your dad at work and ask him from there," Sam said helpfully.

Jessica ran through the Common to the Freeze to use

the phone while Chris ran upstairs to tell Mr. Whitehead about the dog.

Willy and Sam stayed with the dog, who kept thumping its tail against the floor and licking their hands.

In a few minutes, Mr. Whitehead and Jessica's dad were standing with the kids in the closet. Jessica had reached him on his car phone coming home early from work.

"What a sorry-looking mutt!" Mr. Andrews exclaimed, but Jessica could hear the softness in his voice. Her dad really loved animals.

"Could we take him home?" Jessica asked hopefully. "I'll take care of him, Dad. He can be my friend."

Mr. Andrews looked at his daughter and thought for a moment. "Dogs take a lot of work, Jess."

"I know," she said, looking at him pleadingly.

"All right, let's take him home and get him cleaned up." Jessica's dad smiled at his daughter.

"Thank you, Dad!" Jessica cried, giving her dad a big hug.

But the gray dog was too exhausted to get up and refused any coaxing to leave the pile of rags. So the two men slipped a blanket under the dog and carried him out of the church and onto the front seat of the Andrews' car. Jess crawled into the front seat beside the dog, and then she turned and asked the boys to come back to her apartment, too. They all piled into the backseat.

"What'ya going to call him, Jess?" Sam asked.

Jessica secretly wanted to name the dog Leonard, after Mr. Whitehead's first name, but she wasn't sure if he would like having a dog named after him, so she said, "I think I'll call him Thomas, after the man in the diary."

"Thomas . . ." Willy said the name slowly. "It's a people name, but I guess it'll be OK for a dog."

Fortunately the day was very warm, and Thomas got his first bath in a long time under a hose. It took Jessica, Willy, Sam, and Chris well over an hour to clean Thomas's coat of all the mud and tangles. Along the way they managed to get pretty dirty and wet themselves. The dog was pitifully thin under all that thick fur. Jessica's dad called the vet for some advice. The vet told them to feed the dog some cheese at first and then several small meals until Thomas was eating well once again.

For the rest of the week, the Ringers spent a lot of time at Jessica's apartment taking care of Thomas. After a week of such good care, Thomas was eager to go on walks, or actually, "runs." He loved to chase squirrels and rabbits and usually managed to get himself very dirty. Jessica had to give him lots of baths so that he could go to sleep every night on his favorite spot—at the foot of her bed!

It wasn't long before they began calling him the Ringer mascot. Thomas had a part in many of their adventures.

THE END

Turn to page 154.

The next morning they all met back at the church. They were less than excited about Chris's determination to find out what was behind the suspicious man and the kid.

"OK, Chris. What's the plan?" asked Sam.

"Well," said Chris thoughtfully, "let's split up and see if we can see our mystery person. Jill, you and Sam just walk around town. Hang around the Freeze or something. Willy and I will spend the morning at the furniture factory. Meet us at the factory before lunch, and we'll trade places."

"Sounds like a really exciting day," Sam muttered, as he walked away from the church.

"Hey, wait up!" Jill called as she scrambled to run after him.

"Ready?" Chris asked Willy.

CHOICE ⇒

If you want to go with Chris and Willy, turn to page 43.

If you want to go with Jill and Sam, turn to page 57.

Willy, Chris, and Sam crossed the Common quickly and headed toward the Freeze. Just as they were crossing Elm Street, an unshaven man in a brown wrinkled suit burst out of the ice cream parlor and hurriedly crossed the street in the opposite direction. An old baseball cap was pulled down so they couldn't see his eyes.

Willy nodded to the man as they walked past him, but his greeting was ignored. The man was holding a little boy by the hand who was almost running to keep from being dragged. His clothes looked like they hadn't been changed in several days.

As the boys followed the two with their eyes, the little boy glanced back over his shoulder. They could clearly see tears in his eyes. Then his arm was jerked again, and he had to look forward to keep from tripping.

"Wow, that's weird!" said Willy, shaking his head. Sam and Chris just looked at each other and frowned. The two strangers left them with a bad feeling they carried with them into the Freeze.

"Hi, Betty," called Chris as they entered. "Did you notice anything strange about those two who just left here?"

"Yes, I did," answered Betty. "They were standing here like they were going to order while I brought in some milk from the back cooler, and suddenly the man tore out of here like he had seen a ghost!"

"He wasn't very friendly when he went by us, either," said Sam. He had a nagging feeling that they ought to do something about the stranger.

CHOICE

If the boys pursue their suspicions, turn to page 139.

If the boys get back to their adventure with the map, turn to page 63.

"**S**orry I didn't meet you at the old church this morning, Willy."

"What?" exclaimed Willy. "You couldn't get to the church either?"

"'Fraid not," answered Chris. "I forgot to mow the lawn yesterday, so I had to cut it this morning, first thing. Then my mom left a list of chores for me to do today that's a mile long."

"That's too bad," said Willy. "I had to baby-sit Carla, so I couldn't leave this morning either. I wonder if Sam went to the church this morning?"

"Yeah, he did. He just called me to ask me where I was."

"Some adventure we had!" Willy laughed ruefully. "Look, Chris, if you can get through with your chores, and my grandma comes over to baby-sit Carla, maybe we could look for that tunnel this afternoon."

"Sounds good to me," Chris said. "Why don't you call me when your grandmother comes?"

But when the afternoon came, it was Sam's turn to be home handyman so the three boys never did get to the church that day. Instead, Sam invited them over to his house for dinner. Later, they watched a video and spent the night. Exploring the old church for secret passageways would have to wait until the next day.

THE END

If you want to discover another ending to this story, turn to page 94.

Or, turn to page 154.

Jessica had never been very brave. But after reading the diary, she was determined to explore the old church and try to find any secret rooms that had been used to hide slaves.

If the writer of the diary could be brave enough to hide slaves, Jessica told herself, then she should be brave enough to look in a few empty rooms, right? But she wasn't. At least fifty times as she walked to the church the next afternoon, she wanted to turn back. What if she wasn't supposed to explore the old church? No one had actually told her she couldn't, but she still wasn't sure if she should. And she wasn't even sure the church would be open.

She also felt guilty because she had told her dad before he left for work that she had been invited to a friend's house to play. Telling her dad something that wasn't true was bad enough, but to make it even worse, her dad had looked so happy as he had said, "Well, Jess, I'm glad you made a friend!"

That's a joke, Jess thought bitterly. *The kids here have made it very clear that they don't want to be friends with me!*

Finally she reached the church. She was almost disappointed to discover the front door was open. For a long time she stood inside the cool entrance hallway, looking at the animal carvings on the sanctuary doors.

"I wish you could be my friend," she whispered to the lamb. As soon as she had spoken that thought aloud, she felt stupid. *How pathetic, Jess,* she chided herself, *speaking to a door as if it could hear you!*

She finally decided to explore. This time she didn't pull the lamb's ear to open the secret passageway. Instead, she went down to the basement, where the Sunday school rooms were. Reading the diary had made her think that the slaves had been hidden somewhere in the church basement.

Even though the sun was still shining outside, Jessica had brought her flashlight, just in case. Carefully, she opened each of the doors to the Sunday school rooms. Only a part of the basement was actually used on Sunday. Jessica explored that part quickly and then began to look into some of the rooms that had not been used recently for Sunday school.

In one room she saw a huge picture of a man with long hair. She supposed he was Jesus. He was surrounded by sheep and was even carrying one on his shoulders. *Jesus must sure like sheep,* she thought. On the blackboard beside the picture were written the words,

> *I know my sheep, and my sheep know me. I lay down my life for my sheep.*

Now what could that mean? Jessica wondered. *I'll have to remember to ask Mrs. Whitehead next Sunday. I think she really likes sheep, too. She sure talks about them enough.*

Jessica closed the door to the empty Sunday school room and walked back toward the stairs. She was disappointed. *No sign of any secret rooms here,* she thought, *Nothing even remotely interesting. Not even an old book to read.*

She retraced her steps and stood in front of the lamb once more. "I wonder if I should put the diary back," she said to the lamb. "But if I keep it until next Sunday, I could read it one more time for some clues."

CHOICE

If she returns the diary, turn to page 36.

If she waits and reads the diary one more time, turn to page 23.

The three boys raced back to the church. It was afternoon already, and they still hadn't found a way to explore the second tunnel. Willy reached the side door to the basement first.

"You first, Sam," he said with a mock bow.

Sam pushed the stones in and crouched into the darkness. Chris and Willy followed. As their eyes adjusted to the dim light, the three boys saw that both doors at the bottom of the stairs were closed. Sam reached the door to the church basement first and was surprised when it slid quietly upward as soon as he pulled on the ring at the bottom. The stone door behind them swung shut with a faint grumble.

"Hey, I thought you said the door to the church basement was locked, Willy!" Chris exclaimed.

"It was," said Willy, putting his ear to the other door and listening for a moment. He couldn't hear a thing. Maybe he had only been imagining the sounds that morning.

"I guess I'm just extra strong." Sam chuckled as the three boys entered the church basement. Chris pulled the map out of his pocket while Willy turned on the lights in the hallway.

Everything was very quiet in the church. Chris looked at his friends and whispered, "I'm sure glad Mr. Whitehead doesn't mind us exploring around here. Let's make sure we don't mess that up!" Sam and Willy nodded.

"OK, if this map is right," said Chris, walking down the basement hallway, "the second tunnel entrance should be in one of these rooms."

"You mean," Willy added, "if it really is a map!" He couldn't resist teasing his friends.

There were three doors along the left side of the hallway. The boys knew those rooms had never been finished, so there were no lights. They had never paid much attention to those rooms because they could tell from the hallway lights that there was very little in them.

Willy snorted. "Let's look in there," he said, pointing to a door just about the same place as the tunnel entrance should have been.

It was really dark inside the door. Willy pulled out the candle he had brought and the full box of matches. Candlelight gave the room an eerie glow. There was also a damp smell in the room because it hadn't recently been exposed to outside air.

"Yuck, cobwebs," said Willy, feeling the sticky threads on his face.

"And where there's cobwebs, there must be spiders," Chris added.

"I think I just felt one crawl on me," whispered Willy.

"Hey, guys, let's get down to business," Chris suggested.

"OK," said Willy. "What do you think we're looking for?"

Chris thought for a moment, stepped back into the

well-lit hallway to see the map, then said, "There's either a
panel in the wall like the one leading out of the basement
up to the secret side door, or there's a trap door of some
kind, or something."

"Hate to say this, Willy, but that candle doesn't really
give us much light," said Sam. "Where can we get a
flashlight?"

"I've got one at home, but it'll take time to get," said
Chris. "Why don't we just do what we can with the candle,
then come back later with a flashlight?"

Sam wouldn't give up that easily. "I just think that if
we are seriously going to look for a tunnel, we can use all
the light we can get."

Willy felt himself getting stuck in the middle. He
didn't want to wait for a flashlight, but he didn't like the
chances of finding anything by candlelight either.

CHOICE ⇒

If the boys wait for more light, turn to page 56.

If they keep exploring by candlelight, turn to page 11.

The speaker on the police car crackled to life. *"You with the child! This is the police. Stop where you are!"*

At the first sound of the policeman's order, the man jumped as if he had been shot. He spun back from watching Willy and Chris, grabbed the child tightly, and tried to run. But he failed to notice Jill and Sam coming, and he ran right into them. Sam was quick enough to crouch down, causing the man to trip over him. Sam said later it worked better than any block he had ever made in football.

The man instinctively put his hands out as he fell, letting go of the child. The little boy ran right into Jill's arms. He held her so tight she didn't think he'd ever let go. Cursing as he tried to untangle himself from Sam, the stranger forgot for a moment about Officer Gary. He was reminded when the officer grabbed his collar and pulled him to his feet.

"Would you tell these kids to stop bothering me?" yelled the man. "They've been snooping around here, butting in to none of their business."

"Mister, stopping somebody from stealing children is everybody's business," said the policeman as he put handcuffs on the man. Then he informed the man of his rights. The man chose to be angry and silent.

Jill had been kneeling by the boy, who was still

sobbing on her shoulder. The policeman bent over and asked gently, "What's your name, young man?"

The little boy looked at him, then wiped his tears on his dirty sleeve, leaving a brown streak across his face. "Mike Trent," he answered softly.

Jill thought she saw a tear in the corner of the policeman's eye as he said, "This is going to be a great day in your mom and dad's life!" He looked at Jill and added, "Will you walk Mike up to the station while I take this man and lock him up? I don't think Mike would want to be in the same car with him anymore." Jill smiled and nodded.

Behind them, Sam had already explained to Willy and Chris about the mix-up with the pictures and names on the milk cartons. They were jumping and "high-fiving" each other. Now they came over and gathered around Jill, Mike, and the policeman.

Officer Gary cleared his throat and said, "I'm really proud of you kids. And Chris, I'm glad you didn't give up. You're all heroes in my book." Then he added, "I've got another mission for you Ringers. Will you escort Jill and Mike up to the station so we can let him talk to his folks on the phone?"

"Piece of cake!" said Sam.

"Piece of cake?" echoed Willy. "Why did you have to mention food at a time like this? Do you have any idea just how hungry I am?"

As their tight little group began moving up the street, Officer Gary heard Sam ask, "Just *how* hungry are you, Willy?"

"I'm so hungry you can have the piece of cake, and I'll take the rest," said Willy laughing.

130

For a few days, the Ringers were heroes. It felt good to have helped someone else. But they also found out that being heroes has its disadvantages, too. For one thing, people kept asking embarrassing questions. They felt like they were being watched all the time. A week later, the Ringers were glad to be back to normal so they could get on to some adventures that were waiting for them.

THE END

If you haven't read the other adventures in this book, turn to page 104 or 63.

Or, turn to page 154.

"**O**K," said Jessica, surprising even herself as she picked up her purse and followed Chris. When Willy saw her come out of the church beside Chris, she could tell that Willy wasn't very glad to see her. But for once, he made no comment.

"What did you think about ringing the bell this morning?" Sam asked her.

"I loved it!" Jessica exclaimed. "It was wonderful!"

"Well, it was OK," said Willy grudgingly. "But it sure didn't bring many people to church."

"I guess people aren't used to hearing that church bell being rung very often," said Chris.

"That's for sure," said Sam. "Well, what do you guys want to do after lunch?"

Jessica knew she wasn't included in their plans so she hung back a little as they talked.

"What are you going to do this afternoon, Jessica?" asked Sam.

Jessica's face got red because she realized she had been daydreaming. All of the boys were staring at her.

"Mr. Whitehead told me I could explore the picture room at the church," she blurted out. "Do you guys want to come too?"

The question hung in the air for a moment, and nobody said anything. Jessica felt so embarrassed that she began to edge away from the boys. She really didn't know any of them well enough to ask them something like that. And she was usually so shy. She looked down at the sidewalk and wished she hadn't told Chris she would walk home with him. "Well, I've got to go," she mumbled.

As Jessica walked away, the three boys exchanged looks. They knew each other well enough to tell what each other was thinking.

Willy's look plainly said, "No way!"

Sam shrugged as if to say, "Why not give it a try?"

Chris was feeling really guilty because his mom had given him a stern lecture about "moving to a strange town being very hard" and why couldn't he "include Jessica in some of his activities" and "how would he feel if . . ." Chris hadn't exactly listened to the lecture word for word but he had gotten the point.

"OK, Jess," he called to her, ignoring Willy, who looked like a storm ready to happen, "count us in."

She stopped and spun in her tracks, only half believing they had chosen her plan. "Great!" was all she could get out.

"Let's meet back at the church in two hours," Sam suggested. Everyone agreed except Willy, who only grunted. But Sam and Chris knew their friend well enough to know he'd be there. If he could help it, Willy never missed anything that had even the remote possibility of being an adventure!

Exactly two hours later, they met on the stairs of the old church. By now, Jessica felt as if the lamb was an old friend as she watched Sam tug its ear. Single file they all climbed the secret staircase to the picture room.

"What do we look for first?" asked Sam.

"Let's look behind all of the pictures to see if there is, ah, anything else hidden behind them," said Willy exchanging a knowing look with Chris and Sam.

"I want to search through the books," said Jessica, moving toward the shelves on the far wall.

Together the four of them began to search the room. "What a lot of old junk!" Chris exclaimed. "Did you find any secret safes behind those pictures yet, Willy?"

Willy didn't answer but kept on energetically lifting up the old pictures. Sam knelt down by the bookshelves with Jessica and began to look through the old books. He opened one old book and started to read:

> *Breathes there a man with soul so dead,*
> *Who never to himself has said, . . .*

"Oh yuck, poetry!" he groaned. As he was quickly closing that book, a small envelope fell out and fluttered to the floor.

At that same moment Jessica, who had been absorbed in reading a very old hand-written book, looked up in excitement. "Hey, guys, listen to this!"

CHOICE ⇒

If you want to see what's in the envelope that fell out of the book, turn to page 29.

If you want to hear what Jessica discovered, turn to page 53.

"**S**am, are you sure someone's following us?" asked Chris.

"Hey, I know what I saw. Somebody was looking at us from behind a tree when we turned the corner. I just couldn't tell who it was," Sam responded with a slightly irritated whisper.

"Alright," said Chris, leaning toward his friends like a quarterback in the huddle. "Let's do this. I know we're not in trouble with anybody right now, so let's let whoever it is get a little closer, then we'll surprise them by coming back around the corner toward them."

Willy had doubts written all over his face.

Sam elbowed him and said, "Come on, Willy, let's do it!"

Willy gave Sam one of those why-do-I-let-you-talk-me-into-these-things looks and then said, "OK, let's go for it." The tone in his voice let them know that "going for it" was the last thing he wanted to do.

They formed a line several paces back from the corner, and at a silent signal from Chris, they took off running back the way they came. By the time they rounded the corner, all three of them had reached top speed. They leaned into the turn like Olympic athletes. Side by side and stride for stride, they formed a solid wall of speed. It was fun to run!

Unfortunately, they made one minor miscalculation. Whoever was following them was closer than they expected. As Sam, who was next to the building, streaked around the corner, he realized in a flash that someone was *right there!* It was Jill. Instinctively, he swerved to the left to try to miss the girl but then got his feet tangled with Chris's. As the two of them began to fall, they got in Willy's path, and all three ended up in a pile in the grass that grew between the sidewalk and the street.

Jill leaned against the building, laughing until she was weak. "I sure wish I had a videotape of that performance! I'd love to see that in slow motion," she said. "I don't know who was more surprised, me or you."

The boys untangled themselves and made sure they were still all in one piece. "This wasn't my idea, Jill," Willy muttered. "I tried to talk them out of it."

Chris decided it was time to change the subject. "Why were you following us, anyway? You weren't even supposed to be here for a few days," he said to his cousin.

"I decided you Ringers needed a surprise," Jill answered, smiling sweetly all the time. "Besides, don't you remember what day this is?"

"Let me guess," offered Sam. "It's 'Make-a-Fool-of-Yourself-in-Front-of-a-Girl Day'!"

Willy jumped in with a comment. "No, Sam, don't you know it's 'National Grass-Stain Day,'" he said, glancing down at the green streak on his pants.

"You guys are hopeless!" said Jill in exasperation. "Today's my birthday. I've been trying to track you down for a party. Well, maybe not actually a party—it's more like

136

going out for pizza. Now, doesn't that sound better than wherever you were going?"

"We just had lunch," said Chris, still thinking about their plans.

"Lunch?" yelled Willy. "That was at least half an hour ago. I'm already hungry again. Besides, Chris, I think I was just imagining things this morning."

"Yeah," Sam chimed in, "pizza would be nice."

"I guess you guys are right," said Chris with a shrug. But he was a little disappointed.

Jill had been listening with interest. "Wait a minute! What are you guys talking about?"

"We'll tell you all about it on the way to pizza," said Willy as he herded them all back to Chris's apartment. By the time they were wolfing down pizza, Willy had managed to expand his brief minutes in darkness into a major bloodcurdling adventure.

THE END

Turn to page 154.

Chris looked really uncomfortable.

"We can't show you any secret passages today, Jess. We're meeting Sam at his house in about half an hour, and his mom's going to drive us into the city."

I shouldn't have even asked, Jessica thought dejectedly. *They've already made it clear that they don't want me around.*

"But tomorrow," Chris continued, ignoring the glare Willy was giving him, "we could all meet at the church first thing in the morning and see if the passages we've already found match those you've read about in the diary. My cousin Jill is supposed to be here by then, and I'm sure she'll be tagging along with us as well."

"Wha . . . what?" Jessica asked, looking up in confusion.

Chris laughed and repeated what he had just said. Willy didn't look any happier hearing it the second time, but Jessica wasn't looking at Willy.

"Oh, that sounds like fun!" Jessica agreed, trying not to sound too excited.

"See you tomorrow then," Chris called over his shoulder as he and Willy began to walk rapidly toward Sam's house.

Jessica began to walk slowly home, trying to understand what Chris's promise of exploring the old church really meant.

138

Maybe they didn't hate me as much as I thought, she concluded finally. *I'm glad I'm going to finally meet another girl. I hope she likes me! She probably won't be like Mandy, but, I'm sure it's going to be almost impossible to make another friend like Mandy. And maybe by the end of the summer, I'll be able to be a member of the Ringers after all!*

THE END

Turn to page 154.

The boys each ordered their favorite, and Sam leaned against the counter to watch Betty make her magic milk shakes. A silver spout gave her just the amount of chocolate syrup she needed. Next, she pulled out a carton of milk from the cooler.

Sam interrupted her, "Betty, why do you always use milk from a carton when you have that milk dispenser right in front of you?"

She smiled over her shoulder. "I keep the 'two percent' on tap for drinking, but I only use whole milk in my shakes!" she said.

As she poured the milk into the tall shake glasses, Sam noticed something, and his head tilted at the same angle as the milk carton until it seemed he would fall over. When she set the carton back down, Sam's eyes were almost round with surprise. He grabbed Willy and pointed at the carton. "Who does that look like?" he asked.

Willy and Chris leaned forward and stared. Under the word *Missing* printed on the carton was the picture of a little boy who looked exactly like the one they had seen outside just a few minutes ago. The name under the picture read, "Trent Gallagher, age 7."

The three boys looked at each other. "Could it really be?" asked Chris. "Right here in Millersburg?" He remembered the look on the little boy's face, and he suddenly felt like a cold hand was squeezing his stomach. He never enjoyed fear.

"Let's follow them," suggested Willy, forgetting how thirsty he was, "but lets stay sorta far behind them so that they don't see us."

Betty said, "I'm not sure that's such a good idea boys. It could be dangerous. Why don't you call the police first?"

"We'll be careful," said Chris. "We need to find out some information, like where they're staying, before we call the police. If we wait, they may leave town. I think that little boy needs our help."

The boys ran out of the Freeze just in time to catch a glimpse of the man and boy headed up Oak Street. They sprinted in hot pursuit across the Common and saw them turn right again on Pine Street.

"They're heading toward the factory," exclaimed Willy. Everyone called the three story brick building on Pine Street "the factory." At one time about fifty people from Millersburg had worked there making wooden chairs and tables. But the business had long since closed down, and the building was empty.

The boys followed at a distance. When the man had reached the factory, he took a key out of his pocket and crossed the street to a dingy apartment building. People in town called it "the flop house." He hurriedly opened the front door and pulled the little boy inside. The door closed quickly behind them.

"Wow!" Willy exclaimed. "Maybe we should hang around and see if they leave."

"The factory would be a great place to hide and watch the apartment building," Chris pointed out.

"Right," agreed Willy. The boys snuck to the back of the factory and hurriedly climbed the fire escape all the way to the third story. Willy opened the door on the landing and stepped inside. Chris and Sam followed. Scattered across the floor were broken chair parts, overturned crates, dirty papers, and assorted trash. The three boys walked through the mess and stood behind a large broken window that overlooked the street. They could see the apartment building perfectly. If they stood away from the window, no one could see them.

For over an hour they watched the apartment building, but no one came or left.

"This is really boring!" complained Sam. "Willy, are you sure the kid we saw was also on the milk carton?"

"Positive," Willy assured him. "Come on, Sam, you were the one who noticed him first!"

Sometimes, people think they're bored, but they are really just hungry. "I'll go to my house and get us some lunch," suggested Chris. "Then we can eat and keep watching."

"Sounds like a good idea to me," Sam exclaimed.

"Food sounds good to me, too," said Willy.

Chris was back in a flash, and the boys feasted on peanut butter and jelly sandwiches. There was also a can of pop for each.

After lunch, they made a cozy spot for themselves back from the window, and each took turns actually watching.

"Nothing's changed," Willy remarked as Chris walked over to take his place some time later. He was about to sit down by Sam when Chris suddenly jumped to attention.

"Look!" pointed Chris. Both Sam and Willy rushed over and looked down into the street. They saw a tall blond-haired girl advancing cautiously down the street. She kept pausing to peer into the backyards and the spaces between the houses as if she was searching for something.

"Oh, no, Chris," Willy groaned. "It's your cousin."

"Jill wasn't supposed to be here until this weekend," said Chris.

"How did she know we were around here?" wondered Sam.

"I don't know. I guess I'd better go down and see her," said Chris reluctantly.

"Maybe she won't find us if we keep out of sight," Willy suggested hopefully.

CHOICE ⇒

If Chris goes down and talks to Jill, turn to page 38.

If the boys wait and hope Jill doesn't see them, turn to page 40.

They didn't have to ask Jill twice to join them. Moments later they were gathered around the secret side entrance to the church. Because Jill asked, Willy again told briefly how he'd gotten stuck in the tunnel that morning and had been sure someone was down there.

"So we're here to find out if you were right, right?" asked Jill.

"Yeah," added Sam, "and while we're at it we may practice a little kawasaki on them, too."

"What?" asked Jill with a slightly confused frown.

Chris said, "You had to be there, Jill."

The stone door swung open easily, and the gang also found the lower door standing open. They crept down the stairs as quietly as they could. On the way, Willy lit his candle again, this time from a full box of matches. At the bottom of the stairs, Willy turned and put his finger to his lips, asking for silence.

After a moment, Sam whispered, "I don't hear a thing."

Willy said, "Maybe they heard us coming. This could be an ambush!"

"I think your imagination is getting away from you again, Willy," said Jill.

As if determined to prove them wrong, Willy turned and began to work his way along the tunnel. The others followed in single file. (As you will recall if you read about their discovery of this tunnel, it takes two sharp right hand turns before it runs into a rather large open area under the back yard of the church.) When they turned the second corner, all four kids could see that the old door leading into the room was open a crack. There was light in the room.

Hearts beating wildly, the four Ringers tiptoed up to the door. Willy leaned close to the narrow opening and looked through. All he could see was a woman sitting on one of the beds writing something on a yellow pad of paper. The only sound came from the hiss of a lamp creating the light. Willy stepped aside and let each of the others take a peek.

They were so intent on their discovery that they didn't hear a slight noise back in the tunnel.

"Oh, hello, kids!" said a voice behind them.

The surprise was complete. Four bodies jumped as if the floor had just exploded. Willy's candle almost went out again.

"Well, I didn't mean to frighten you," said the friendly voice of Mr. Whitehead out of the darkness. "You kind of surprised me, too. I was just thinking about you." He stepped into the circle of candlelight with a big smile on his face.

A woman's voice called out from the room. "Mr. Whitehead, is that you?"

"Yes, it is," Mr. Whitehead called out. "And I've brought some guests." He motioned the kids to go in. As they filed into the room, he continued, "These are some of those famous Ringers I was telling you about. They discovered this tunnel on their own. And they've made some other discoveries around here, too." He paused and then made some formal introductions. It turned out the woman was Mrs. Alice Turner, a historian who was doing research for a book on the Underground Railroad.

Willy said, "My great-grandmother talks about the Underground Railroad all the time. Her grandfather used it to get his freedom."

"Well, Willy, Mrs. Turner is almost sure that the church was used as a station for slaves like your ancestor trying to escape to freedom before and during the Civil War," explained Mr. Whitehead.

"You could all help me a lot by telling me what you have found so far," said Mrs. Turner in a friendly way. She then said in a more serious tone, "I know that these tunnels are important secrets for you, but you need to know that the tunnels are important to a lot of other people for a different reason."

CHOICE

Turn to page 30.

The noises from the tunnel below him were getting louder. It almost sounded as if someone was dragging something across the floor. Willy thought he heard someone talking rapidly, but he couldn't understand the words.

For a long time Willy listened to the sounds. He sat down in the darkness with his back against the wall, staring in the direction of the door at the bottom of the stairs. Without warning, the outside door flew open. Light flooded the stairway.

"Hey, Willy, what are you doing here in the dark?"

Willy instantly recognized Chris's voice. He jumped to his feet and stumbled out into the sunshine. Chris followed him. Willy felt like giving him a big hug, but he wasn't sure if his friend would understand.

"Willy, are you OK? You look kinda scared," Chris asked.

"I'm OK. The door stuck, and I couldn't get out. I kept thinking I heard some funny noises coming from the tunnel. Where were you guys? We were supposed to explore the tunnel today, remember?"

"We got held up at Sam's house. So, we went to your house to see where you were. Your sister got pretty scared when she heard us at the door. When she saw it was us, she let us in and showed us your note."

"Where's Sam?"

"He stayed behind with Carla," Chris said as he looked sideways at his friend. "Uh, Willy, you know Carla's pretty little to be left alone."

"Yeah, I know," Willy said sheepishly. "It was really dumb to leave her like that after my Mom told me to watch her. I thought about that a lot when I was trapped in the tunnel. I'm just lucky that you came."

"Come on," said Chris, seeing how guilty his friend felt. "I'll race you back to the apartment."

Willy and Chris dashed all the way to Willy's apartment. Willy ran into the kitchen, picked up Carla, and gave her a big hug.

"I was really scared, Willy," said Carla. Willy looked at her face and could tell that she had been crying.

"So was I," admitted Willy, "and I'm really sorry that I left you alone. I won't do it again, OK?"

Carla nodded solemnly.

Just then the phone rang, and Willy answered it.

He listened for a moment, smiled, then hung up. "Carla, it's Grandma," Willy exclaimed. "She says that she'll be here in a few minutes, and she's bringing ice cream for dessert at lunch!"

"Hurray!" Carla shouted.

"When she gets here, we'll eat and then head back to the church," Willy suggested to his friends. Their nods told him they liked the plan.

A little while later, the phone rang again. This time it was Willy's mom.

"How are things going, Son?"

"OK, Mom," Willy paused, "now."

"Now?"

"Yeah, I had a little problem this morning, but everything's OK now."

"What kind of problem?" Willy's mom asked.

"I'll tell you about it when you come home, OK?"

"OK, Willy. You know, I'm so glad I never have to worry about Carla when you're watching her."

Willy gulped. He really wanted that to be true. "Thanks, Mom," he said.

A short time later, Grandma walked in the door.

"Grandma!" Carla shouted as she hugged and kissed her.

After everyone had said hello, Willy's grandma went into the kitchen to fix them some lunch.

It was the first chance the boys had to talk about Willy's experience that morning. He tried to convince them he really had heard something or someone down in the tunnel.

"I thought we were the only ones who knew about it," said Sam thoughtfully.

Chris added, "Are you sure you weren't just hearing things because you were scared?"

"Well, I wasn't *that* scared," said Willy a little defensively.

"Maybe we should check that tunnel out before we look for the new one," suggested Chris, not wanting to hurt Willy's feelings. Besides, it would only take a few minutes.

"I hope that doesn't take too long," said Sam. "It could

take us a while to figure out where the entrance to that other tunnel is. What if the opening is really hidden?"

"Or what if the map turns out to be nothing but somebody's doodles?" said Willy, still kidding his friends.

CHOICE

If the boys check out Willy's story, turn to page 110.

If they just try to find the other tunnel, turn to page 125.

Willy and Sam waited impatiently in the furniture factory. They took turns watching the window while the other person explored a little of the factory.

Willy found an old tennis shoe and an empty Coke can. Sam found a dusty bird's nest that had fallen to the floor, a funny looking empty blue bottle, and a pack of cards. Sam was excited about the bottle because his Aunt Stella collected them. He cleaned it off on his shirt and wrapped the bottle in an old rag to take to Aunt Stella as a present. Willy was excited about the cards because he was really bored just watching a building.

They played several games of 500 Rummy until finally they heard Jill and Chris coming up the back stairs. Willy and Sam were anxious. "Where are the cops?" asked Willy.

"They're not coming," answered Jill.

"This kid Trent got found just a few days ago. So the one we saw can't be the one on the milk carton," added Chris. "But I'm still not sure about what's going on here," he continued, nodding toward the apartment.

Sam tried to be helpful. "Maybe we were all letting our imaginations run away with us! I think we should forget this wild goose chase. After all, we did find that map yesterday, and we haven't even had a chance to check it out!"

"What map?" asked Jill.

"Oh, nothing. Just a piece of paper with squiggles on it," said Willy, smirking at Chris.

Chris wasn't listening. He was making up his mind to do something. "Look, you guys, I think this is serious," he said. "I'm not ready to quit. We have a possible kidnapping here. Let's meet right here tomorrow morning first thing and see what we can do!"

The others looked at each other, trying to decide what they should do.

CHOICE ⇒

If they decide that "Trent Gallagher" was kidnapped, turn to page 117.

If they decide it's time to check out the map, turn to page 33.

It was one of those times when a decision had to be made. If they waited too long, whoever was following them would show up. They actually all made the decision together. Suddenly, they were running. Running like their lives depended on it. Quickly, they reached the hedge of tall evergreens where they would turn to pass along the side of the church to the secret entrance. Sam was slightly in the lead.

Suddenly, from behind the bushes, a girl jumped out with a shout, "Hold it!"

The boys were completely taken by surprise. They tried to stop in their tracks but managed to collide with each other like the Keystone Cops. The girl couldn't help chuckling at them.

"Jill!" said Chris, glaring at his cousin. He had to admit she had really surprised them, but he was a little upset at her for doing it, too. "I didn't think you'd be here for a few days," he said.

"We decided to show up early," Jill answered, still clearly enjoying herself. "I'm glad I did, just so I could make life a little more interesting for you." She saw they had no snappy answers, so she continued, "So, where were you guys going?"

CHOICE ➤

If the boys let Jill in on their plans, turn to page 143.

If the boys try to keep their plans from Jill, turn to page 73.

If you have read all the adventures in this book, you should have figured out two mysteries before the gang does. First, you know from the sign in the second tunnel why the dirt filled the doorway in the first tunnel. Second, you know how the tunnel that begins in the field and the one that begins in the back room of the church basement are connected. Figuring that out makes you a Ringer, too!

An old diary has played an important part in several of the adventures in this book. Do you want to keep a journal, or diary, like the one Jessica found? All you need is a pencil and a notebook or some pages of blank paper. Every few days, or every day if you want, just write down some of the things that happen to you and your friends. Don't forget to include your thoughts and feelings, and most important, your dreams!

Your own adventures are really important, too. Why not write them down in a special book that is just yours to read? You'll have to find a good hiding place! Jessica hid hers under the mattress, but I'm sure you can think of some other hiding places! Good luck and have fun! Who knows who might discover your journal some day!

Sally Marcey is a pastor's wife and mother of two children. Her interest in creative fiction is reflected in making up her children's bedtime stories for years. She also teaches Sunday school.

*If you enjoy **Choice Adventures**, you'll
want to read these exciting series from
Tyndale House Publishers!*

You can find Tyndale books at fine bookstores everywhere.
If you are unable to find these titles at your local bookstore,
you may write for ordering information to:

**Tyndale House Publishers
Tyndale Family Products Dept.
Box 448
Wheaton, IL 60189**